"A master storyteller."

—Washington Times

"McBain is a skillful writer who excels at pace, plot, and, especially, the complex clockwork of a cop's mind."

—People

"I never read Ed McBain without the awful thought that I still have a lot to learn. And when you think you're catching up, he gets better." *—Tony Hillerman*

"McBain has a great approach, great attitude, terrific style, strong plots, excellent dialogue, sense of place, and sense of reality." *—Elmore Leonard*

"Nobody writes better detective fiction than Ed McBain. Nobody." *—West Coast Review of Books*

"McBain's characters age, change, and stay interesting."

—Arizona Daily Star

"McBain is the unquestioned king. . . . Light-years ahead of anyone else in the field." *—San Diego Union-Tribune*

"No living mystery writer creates more suspenseful scenes or builds plots better than McBain."

—Greensboro News & Record

ED McBAIN

FUZZ

WARNER BOOKS

A Time Warner Company

The city in these pages is imaginary. The people, the places, are all fictitious. Only the police routine is based on established investigatory technique.

WARNER BOOKS EDITION

Cover design and art by Tony Greco

Warner Books, Inc.
1271 Avenue of the Americas
New York, NY 10020

Visit our Web site at
www.twbookmark.com

 A Time Warner Company

Printed in the United States of America

First Paperback Printing: December 2000

10 9 8 7 6 5 4 3 2 1

This is for my father-in-law,
Harry Melnick,
who inspired *The Heckler*,
and who must therefore take
at least partial blame for this one.

Fuzz

OH BOY, WHAT A WEEK.

Fourteen muggings, three rapes, a knifing on Culver Avenue, thirty-six assorted burglaries, and the squadroom was being painted.

Not that the squadroom didn't *need* painting.

Detective Meyer Meyer would have been the first man to admit that the squadroom definitely needed painting. It merely seemed idiotic for the city to decide to paint it now, at the beginning of March, when everything outside was rotten and cold and miserable and dreary, and when you had to keep the windows shut tight because you never could get enough damn heat up in the radiators, and as a result had the stink of turpentine in your nostrils all day long, not to mention two painters underfoot and overhead, both of whom never would have made it in the Sistine Chapel.

"Excuse me," one of the painters said, "could you move that thing?"

"What thing?" Meyer said.

"That thing."

"*That* thing," Meyer said, almost blowing his cool, "happens to be our Lousy File. *That* thing happens to contain information on known criminals and trouble-makers in the precinct, and *that* thing happens to be invaluable to the hard-working detectives of this squad."

"Big deal," the painter said.

"Won't he move it?" the other painter asked.

"You move it," Meyer said. "You're the painters, *you* move it."

"We're not supposed to move nothing," the first painter said.

"We're only supposed to paint," the second painter said.

"I'm not supposed to move things, either," Meyer said. "I'm supposed to detect."

"Okay, so don't move it," the first painter said, "it'll get all full of green paint."

"Put a dropcloth on it," Meyer said.

"We got our dropcloths over there on those desks there," the second painter said, "that's all the dropcloths we got."

"Why is it I always get involved with vaudeville acts?" Meyer asked.

"Huh?" the first painter said.

"He's being wise," the second painter said.

"All I know is I don't plan to move that filing cabinet," Meyer said. "In fact, I don't plan to move *any-*

thing. You're screwing up the whole damn squadroom, we won't be able to find anything around here for a week after you're gone."

"We do a thorough job," the first painter said.

"Besides, we didn't ask to come," the second painter said. "You think we got nothing better to do than shmear around up here? You think this is an interesting job or something? This is a *boring* job, if you want to know."

"It is, huh?" Meyer said.

"Yeah, it's boring," the second painter said.

"It's boring, that's right," the first painter agreed.

"Everything apple green, you think that's interesting? The ceiling apple green, the walls apple green, the stairs apple green, that's some interesting job, all right."

"We had a job last week at the outdoor markets down on Council Street, *that* was an interesting job."

"That was the most interesting job we ever had," the second painter said. "Every stall was a different pastel color, you know those stalls they got? Well, every one of them was a different pastel color, *that* was a *good* job."

"*This* is a *crappy* job." the first painter said.

"It's boring and it's crappy," the second painter agreed.

"I'm still not moving that cabinet," Meyer said, and the telephone rang. "87th Squad, Detective Meyer," he said into the receiver.

"Is this Meyer Meyer in person?" the voice on the other end asked.

"Who's this?" Meyer asked.

"First please tell me if I'm speaking to Meyer Meyer himself?"

"This is Meyer Meyer himself."

"Oh God, I think I may faint dead away."

"Listen, who . . ."

"This is Sam Grossman."

"Hello, Sam, what's . . ."

"I can't tell you how thrilled I am to be talking to such a famous person," Grossman said.

"Yeah?"

"Yeah."

"Okay, what is it? I don't get it."

"You mean you don't know?"

"No, I don't know. What is it I'm supposed to know?" Meyer asked.

"I'm sure you'll find out," Grossman said.

"There's nothing I hate worse than a mystery," Meyer said, "so why don't you just tell me what you're talking about and save me a lot of trouble?"

"Ah-ha," Grossman said.

"You I need today," Meyer said, and sighed.

"Actually, I'm calling about a man's sports jacket, size thirty-eight, color red-and-blue plaid, label Tom's Town and Country, analysis of suspect stain on the left front flap requested. Know anything about it?"

"I requested the test," Meyer said.

"You got a pencil handy?"

"Shoot."

"Blood negative, semen negative. Seems to be an ordinary kitchen stain, grease or oil. You want us to break it down?"

"No, that won't be necessary."

"This belong to a rape suspect?"

"We've had three dozen rape suspects in here this week. We also have two painters."

"I beg your pardon?"

"Forget it. Is that all?"

"That's all. It certainly was a pleasure talking to you, Mr. Meyer Meyer, you have no idea how thrilled I am."

"Listen, what the hell . . .?" Meyer started, but Grossman hung up. Meyer held the receiver in his hand a moment longer, looking at it peculiarly, and then put it back onto the cradle. He noticed that there were several spatters of apple green paint on the black plastic. "God-damn slobs," he muttered under his breath, and one of the painters said, "What?"

"Nothing."

"I thought you said something."

"Listen, what department are you guys from, anyway?" Meyer asked.

"Public Works," the first painter said.

"Maintenance and Repair," the second painter said.

"Whyn't you come paint this damn place last summer, instead of now when all the windows are closed?"

"Why? What's the matter?"

"It stinks in here, that's what's the matter," Meyer said.

"It stunk in here even before we got here," the first painter said, which was perhaps true. Meyer sniffed disdainfully, turned his back on the two men, and tried to locate the filing cabinet containing last week's D.D. reports, which cabinet seemed to have vanished from sight.

If there was one thing (and there were *many* things) Meyer could not abide, it was chaos. The squadroom was in a state of utter, complete, and total chaos. Stepladders, dropcloths, newspapers, closed paint cans, open paint cans, used paint brushes, clean paint brushes, cans of turpentine and cans of thinner, mixing sticks, color samples (all in various lovely shades of apple green), rollers, rolling trays, rolls of masking tape, coveralls, stained rags were strewn, thrown, draped, scattered, leaning against, lying upon, spread over and balanced precariously on desks, cabinets, floors, walls, water coolers, window sills, and anything inanimate. (Yesterday, the painters had almost thrown a dropcloth over the inert form of Detective Andy Parker who was, as usual, asleep in the swivel chair behind his desk, his feet propped up on an open drawer.) Meyer stood in the midst of this disorder like the monument to patience he most certainly was, a sturdy man with china blue eyes and a bald head, speckled now (he didn't even realize it) with apple green paint. There was a pained look on his round face, his shoulders slumped with fatigue, he seemed disoriented and discombobulated, and he didn't know where the hell anything *was!* Chaos, he thought, and the telephone rang again.

He was standing closest to Carella's desk, so he groped around under the dropcloth for the ringing telephone, came away with a wide apple green stain on his jacket sleeve, and bounded across the room to the phone on his own desk. Swearing, he lifted the receiver.

"87th Squad, Detective Meyer," he said.

"Parks Commissioner Cowper will be shot to death

tomorrow night unless I receive five thousand dollars before noon," a man's voice said. "More later."

"What?" Meyer said.

The line went dead.

He looked at his watch. It was four-fifteen P.M.

At four-thirty that afternoon, when Detective Steve Carella got to the squadroom, Lieutenant Byrnes asked him to come to his office for a moment. He was sitting behind his desk in the two-windowed room, puffing on a cigar and looking very much like a boss (which he was) in his gray pin-striped suit, a shade darker than his close-cropped hair, a black-and-gold silk rep tie on his white shirt (tiny spatter of apple green on one cuff), college ring with maroon stone on his right ring finger, wedding band on his left. He asked Carella if he wanted a cup of coffee, and Carella said yes, and Byrnes buzzed Miscolo in the Clerical Office and asked him to bring in another cup of coffee, and then asked Meyer to fill Carella in on the telephone call. It took Meyer approximately ten seconds to repeat the content of the conversation.

"Is that it?" Carella asked.

"That's it."

"Mmm."

"What do you think, Steve?" Byrnes asked.

Carella was sitting on the edge of Byrnes' scarred desk, a tall slender man who looked like a vagrant at the moment because as soon as it got dark he would take to the streets, find himself an alley or a doorway and lie there reeking of wine and hoping somebody would set fire to him. Two weeks ago, a *real* vagrant had been set ablaze by some fun-loving youngsters, and last week another bum had supplied fuel for a second bonfire, a fatal one this time. So Carella had been spending his nights lying in assorted doorways simulating drunkenness and wishing for arson. He had not shaved for three days. There was a bristly stubble on his jaw, the same color as his brown hair, but growing in sparsely and patchily and giving his face a somewhat incomplete look, as though it had been hastily sketched by an inexpert artist. His eyes were brown (he liked to think of them as penetrating), but they appeared old and faded now through association with the scraggly beard and the layers of unadulterated dirt he had allowed to collect on his forehead and his cheeks. What appeared to be a healing cut ran across the bridge of his nose, collodion and vegetable dye skillfully applied to resemble congealing blood and pus and corruption. He also looked as if he had lice. He made Byrnes a little itchy. He made everybody in the room a little itchy. He blew his nose before answering the lieutenant's question, and the handkerchief he took from the back pocket of his greasy pants looked as if it had been fished from a nearby sewer. He blew his nose fluidly (there's such a thing as carrying an impersonation *too* far, Meyer thought), replaced the handkerchief in his trouser pocket, and then said, "He ask to talk to anyone in particular?"

"Nope, just began talking the minute I said who I was."

"Could be a crank," Carella said.

"Could be."

"Why *us?*" Byrnes said.

It was a good question. Assuming the man was *not* a crank, and assuming he *did* plan to kill the commissioner of parks unless he got his five thousand dollars by noon tomorrow, why call the Eight-Seven? There were a great many squadrooms in this fair city, none of which (it was safe to assume) were in the midst of being painted that first week in March, all of which contained detectives every bit as hard-working and determined as the stalwart fellows who gathered together now to sip their afternoon beverages and while away the deepening hours, all of whom doubtless knew the commissioner of parks as intimately as did these very minions of the law—so why the Eight-Seven?

A good question. Like most good questions, it was not immediately answered. Miscolo came in with a cup of coffee, asked Carella when he planned to take a bath, and then went back to his clerical duties. Carella picked up the coffee cup in a filth-encrusted hand, brought it to his cracked and peeling lips, sipped at it, and then said, "We ever having anything to do with Cowper?"

"How do you mean?"

"I don't know. Any special assignments, anything like that?"

"Not to my recollection," Byrnes said. "Only thing I can think of is when he spoke at that P.B.A. thing, but every cop in the city was invited to that one."

"It must be a crank," Carella said.

"Could be," Meyer said again.

"Did he sound like a kid?" Carella asked.

"No, he sounded like a grown man."

"Did he say when he'd call again?"

"No. All he said was 'More later.'"

"Did he say when or where you were supposed to deliver the money?"

"Nope."

"Did he say where you were supposed to *get* it?"

"Nope."

"Maybe he expects us to take up a collection," Carella said.

"Five grand is only five hundred and fifty dollars less than I make in a year," Meyer said.

"Sure, but he's undoubtedly heard how generous the bulls of the 87th are."

"I admit he sounds like a crank," Meyer said. "Only one thing bothers me about what he said."

"What's that?"

"Shot to death. I don't like that, Steve. Those words scare me."

"Yeah. Well," Carella said, "why don't we see if he calls again, okay? Who's relieving?"

"Kling and Hawes should be in around five."

"Who's on the team?" Byrnes asked.

"Willis and Brown. They're relieving on post."

"Which case?"

"Those car snatches. They're planted on Culver and Second."

"You think it's a crank, Meyer?"

"It could be. We'll have to see."

"Should we call Cowper?"

"What for?" Carella said. "This may turn out to be nothing. No sense alarming him."

"Okay," Byrnes said. He looked at his watch, rose, walked to the hatrack in the corner, and put on his overcoat. "I promised Harriet I'd take her shopping, the stores are open late tonight. I should be home around nine if anybody wants to reach me. Who'll be catching?"

"Kling."

"Tell him I'll be home around nine, will you?"

"Right."

"I hope it's a crank," Byrnes said, and went out of the office.

Carella sat on the edge of the desk, sipping his coffee. He looked very tired. "How does it feel to be famous?" he asked Meyer.

"What do you mean?"

Carella looked up. "Oh, I guess you don't know yet."

"Don't know *what* yet?"

"About the book."

"What book?"

"Somebody wrote a book."

"So?"

"It's called *Meyer Meyer.*"

"What?"

"Yeah. *Meyer Meyer.* It was reviewed in today's paper."

"Who? What do you mean? Meyer *Meyer,* you mean?"

"It got a nice review."

"Meyer Meyer?" Meyer said. "That's *my* name."

"Sure."

"He can't do that!"

"She. A woman."

"Who?"

"Her name's Helen Hudson."

"She can't do that!"

"She's already done it."

"Well, she *can't*. I'm a *person*, you can't go naming some character after a *person*." He frowned and then looked at Carella suspiciously. "Are you putting me on?"

"Nope, God's honest truth."

"Is this guy supposed to be a cop?"

"No, I think he's a teacher."

"A *teacher*, Jesus Christ!"

"At a university."

"She can't do that!" Meyer said again. "Is he bald?"

"I don't know. He's short and plump, the review said."

"Short and plump! She can't use my name for a short plump person. I'll sue her."

"So sue her," Carella said.

"You think I won't? Who published that goddamn book?"

"Dutton."

"Okay!" Meyer said, and took a pad from his jacket pocket. He wrote swiftly on a clean white page, slammed the pad shut, dropped it to the floor as he was putting it back into his pocket, swore, stooped to pick it up, and then looked at Carella plaintively and said, "After all, *I* was here first."

The second call came at ten minutes to eleven that night. It was taken by Detective Bert Kling, who was catching, and who had been briefed on the earlier call before Meyer left the squadroom.

"87th Squad," he said, "Kling here."

"You've undoubtedly decided by now that I'm a crank," the man's voice said. "I'm not."

"Who is this?" Kling asked, and motioned across the room for Hawes to pick up the extension.

"I was quite serious about what I promised," the man said. "Parks Commissioner Cowper will be shot to death sometime tomorrow night unless I receive five thousand dollars by noon. This is how I want it. Have you got a pencil?"

"Mister, why'd you pick on *us?*" Kling asked.

"For sentimental reasons," the man said, and Kling could have sworn he was smiling on the other end of the line. "Pencil ready?"

"Where do you expect us to get five thousand dollars?"

"Entirely your problem," the man said. "*My* problem is killing Cowper if you fail to deliver. Do you want this information?"

"Go ahead," Kling said, and glanced across the room to where Hawes sat hunched over the other phone. Hawes nodded.

"I want the money in singles, need I mention they must be unmarked?"

"Mister, do you know what extortion is?" Kling asked suddenly.

"I know what it is," the man said. "Don't try keeping me on the line. I plan to hang up long before you can effect a trace."

"Do you know the penalty for extortion?" Kling asked, and the man hung up.

"*Son* of a bitch," Kling said.

"He'll call back. We'll be ready next time," Hawes said.

"We can't trace it through automatic equipment, anyway."

"We can try."

"*What'd* he say?"

"He said 'sentimental reasons.' "

"That's what I thought he said. What's that supposed to mean?"

"Search me," Hawes said, and went back to his desk, where he had spread a paper towel over the dropcloth, and where he had been drinking tea from a cardboard container and eating a cheese Danish before the telephone call interrupted him.

He was a huge man, six feet two inches and weighing two hundred pounds, some ten pounds more than was comfortable for him. He had blue eyes and a square jaw with a cleft chin. His hair was red, except for a streak over his left temple where he had once been knifed and where the hair had curiously grown in white after the wound healed. He had a straight unbroken nose, and a good mouth with a wide lower lip. Sipping his tea, munching his Danish, he looked like a burly Captain Ahab who had somehow been trapped in a civil service job. A gun butt protruded from the holster under his coat as he leaned over the paper towel and allowed the Danish crumbs to fall onto it. The gun was a big one, as befitted the size of the man, a Smith & Wesson .357 Magnum, weighing 44 ½ ounces, and capable of putting a hole the size of a baseball in your head if you happened to cross the path of Cotton Hawes on a night when the moon was full. He was biting into the Danish when the telephone rang again.

"87th Squad, Kling here."

"The penalty for extortion," the man said, "is imprisonment not exceeding fifteen years. Any other questions?"

"Listen . . ." Kling started.

"*You* listen," the man said. "I want five thousand dollars in unmarked singles. I want them put into a metal lunch pail, and I want the pail taken to the third bench on the Clinton Street footpath into Grover Park. More later," he said, and hung up.

"We're going to play Fits and Starts, I see," Kling said to Hawes.

"Yeah. Shall we call Pete?"

"Let's wait till we have the whole picture," Kling said, and sighed and tried to get back to typing up his report. The phone did not ring again until eleven-twenty. When he lifted the receiver, he recognized the man's voice at once.

"To repeat," the man said, "I want the lunch pail taken to the third bench on the Clinton Street footpath into Grover Park. If the bench is watched, if your man is not alone, the pail will not be picked up, and the commissioner will be killed."

"You want five grand left on a park bench?" Kling asked.

"You've got it," the man said, and hung up.

"You think that's all of it?" Kling asked Hawes.

"I don't know," Hawes said. He looked up at the wall

clock. "Let's give him till midnight. If we don't get another call by then, we'll ring Pete."

"Okay," Kling said.

He began typing again. He typed hunched over the machine, using a six-finger system that was uniquely his own, typing rapidly and with a great many mistakes, overscoring or erasing as the whim struck him, detesting the paperwork that went into police work, wondering why anyone would want a metal pail left on a park bench where any passing stranger might pick it up, cursing the decrepit machine provided by the city, and then wondering how anyone could have the unmitigated gall to demand five thousand dollars *not* to commit a murder. He frowned as he worked, and because he was the youngest detective on the squad, with a face comparatively unravaged by the pressures of his chosen profession, the only wrinkle in evidence was the one caused by the frown, a deep cutting ridge across his smooth forehead. He was a blond man, six feet tall, with hazel eyes and an open countenance. He wore a yellow sleeveless pullover, and his brown sports jacket was draped over the back of his chair. The Colt .38 Detective's Special he usually wore clipped to his belt was in its holster in the top drawer of his desk.

He took seven calls in the next half-hour, but none of them were from the man who had threatened to kill Cowper. He was finishing his report, a routine listing of the persons interrogated in a mugging on Ainsley Avenue, when the telephone rang again. He reached for the receiver automatically. Automatically, Hawes lifted the extension.

"Last call tonight," the man said. "I want the money before noon tomorrow. There are more than one of us, so don't attempt to arrest the man who picks it up or the commissioner will be killed. If the lunch pail is empty, or if it contains paper scraps or phony bills or marked bills, or if for any reason or by any circumstance the money is not on that bench before noon tomorrow, the plan to kill the commissioner will go into effect. If you have any questions, ask them now."

"You don't really expect us to hand you five thousand dollars on a silver platter, do you?"

"No, in a lunch pail," the man said, and again Kling had the impression he was smiling.

"I'll have to discuss this with the lieutenant," Kling said.

"Yes, and he'll doubtless have to discuss it with the parks commissioner," the man said.

"Is there any way we can reach you?" Kling asked, taking a wild gamble, thinking the man might hastily and automatically reveal his home number or his address.

"You'll have to speak louder," the man said. "I'm a little hard of hearing."

"I said is there any way . . ."

And the man hung up.

The bitch city can intimidate you sometimes by her size alone, but when she works in tandem with the weather she can make you wish you were dead. Cotton Hawes wished he was dead on that Tuesday, March 5. The temperature as recorded at the Grover Park Lake at seven A.M. that morning was twelve degrees above zero, and by nine A.M.—when he started onto the Clinton Street footpath—it had risen only two degrees to stand at a frigid fourteen above. A strong harsh wind was blowing off the River Harb to the north, racing untrammeled through the narrow north-south corridor leading directly to the path. His red hair whipped fitfully about his hat-less head, the tails of his overcoat were flat against the backs of his legs. He was wearing gloves and carrying a black lunch pail in his left hand. The third button of his overcoat, waist high, was open, and the butt of his Magnum rested just behind the gaping flap, ready for a quick right-handed, spring-assisted draw.

The lunch pail was empty.

They had awakened Lieutenant Byrnes at five minutes to twelve the night before, and advised him of their subsequent conversations with the man they now referred to as The Screwball. The lieutenant had mumbled a series of grunts into the telephone and then said, "I'll be right down," and then asked what time it was. They told him it was almost midnight. He grunted again, and hung up. When he got to the squadroom, they filled him in more completely, and it was decided to call the parks commissioner to apprise him of the threat against his life, and to discuss any possible action with him. The parks commissioner looked at his bedside clock the moment the phone rang and immediately informed Lieutenant Byrnes that it was half past midnight, wasn't this something that could wait until morning?

Byrnes cleared his throat and said, "Well, someone says he's going to shoot you."

The parks commissioner cleared his throat and said, "Well, why didn't you say so?"

The situation was ridiculous.

The parks commissioner had never heard of a more ridiculous situation, why this man had to be an absolute maniac to assume anyone would pay him five thousand dollars on the strength of a few phone calls. Byrnes agreed that the situation was ridiculous, but that nonetheless a great many crimes in this city were committed daily by misguided or unprincipled people, some of whom were doubtless screwballs, but sanity was not a prerequisite for the successful perpetration of a criminal act.

The situation was unthinkable.

The parks commissioner had never heard of a more unthinkable situation, he couldn't even understand why they were bothering him with what were obviously the rantings of some kind of lunatic. Why didn't they simply forget the entire matter?

"Well," Byrnes said, "I hate to behave like a television cop, sir, I would really *rather* forget the entire thing, as you suggest, but the possibility exists that there *is* a plan to murder you, and in all good conscience I cannot ignore that possibility, not without discussing it first with you."

"Well, you've discussed it with me," the parks commissioner said, "and I say forget it."

"Sir," Byrnes said, "we would like to try to apprehend the man who picks up the lunch pail, and we would also like to supply you with police protection tomorrow night. Had you planned on leaving the house tomorrow night?"

The parks commissioner said that Byrnes could do whatever he thought fit in the matter of apprehending the man who picked up the lunch pail, but that he did indeed plan on going out tomorrow night, was in fact invited by the mayor to attend a performance of Beethoven's *Eroica* given by the Philharmonic at the city's recently opened music and theater complex near Remington Circle, and he did not want or need police protection.

Byrnes said, "Well, sir, let's see what results we have with the lunch pail, we'll get back to you."

"Yes, get back to me," the parks commissioner said, "but not in the middle of the night again, okay?" and hung up.

At five A.M. on Tuesday morning while it was still dark, Detectives Hal Willis and Arthur Brown drank two fortifying cups of coffee in the silence of the squadroom, donned foul-weather gear requisitioned from an Emergency Squad truck, clipped on their holsters, and went out onto the arctic tundra to begin a lonely surveillance of the third bench on the Clinton Street footpath into Grover Park. Since most of the park's paths meandered from north to south and naturally had entrances on either end, they thought at first there might be some confusion concerning the Clinton Street footpath. But a look at the map on the precinct wall showed that there was only one entrance to this particular path, which began on Grover Avenue, adjacent to the park, and then wound through the park to end at the band shell near the lake. Willis and Brown planted themselves on a shelf of rock overlooking the suspect third bench, shielded from the path by a stand of naked elms. It was very cold. They did not expect action, of course, until Hawes dropped the lunch pail where specified, but they could hardly take up posts after the event, and so it had been Byrnes' brilliant idea to send them out before anyone watching the bench might observe them. They did windmill exercises with their arms, they stamped their feet, they continuously pressed the palms of their hands against portions of their face that seemed to be going, the telltale whiteness of frostbite appearing suddenly and frighteningly in the bleak early morning hours. Neither of the two men had ever been so cold in his life.

Cotton Hawes was almost, but not quite, as cold when he entered the park at nine A.M. that morning. He passed two people on his way to the bench. One of them was an old man in a black overcoat, walking swiftly toward the subway kiosk on Grover Avenue. The other was a girl wearing a mink coat over a long pink nylon nightgown that flapped dizzily about her ankles, walking a white poodle wearing a red wool vest. She smiled at Hawes as he went by with his lunch pail.

The third bench was deserted.

Hawes took a quick look around and then glanced up and out of the park to the row of apartment buildings on Grover Avenue. A thousand windows reflected the early morning sun. Behind any one of those windows, there might have been a man with a pair of binoculars and a clear unobstructed view of the bench. He put the lunch pail on one end of the bench, moved it to the other end, shrugged, and relocated it in the exact center of the bench. He took another look around, feeling really pretty stupid, and then walked out of the park and back to the office. Detective Bert Kling was sitting at his desk, monitoring the walkie-talkie operated by Hal Willis in the park.

"How you doing down there?" Kling asked.

"We're freezing our asses off," Willis replied.

"Any action yet?"

"You think anybody's crazy enough to be out in this weather?" Willis said.

"Cheer up," Kling said, "I hear the boss is sending you both to Jamaica when this is over."

"Fat Chance Department," Willis said. "Hold it!"

There was silence in the squadroom. Hawes and Kling waited. At last, Willis' voice erupted from the speaker on Kling's box.

"Just a kid," Willis said. "Stopped at the bench, looked over the lunch pail, and then left it right where it was."

"Stay with it," Kling said.

"We have to stay with it," Brown's voice cut in. "We're frozen solid to this goddamn rock."

There were people in the park now.

They ventured into the bitch city tentatively, warned by radio and television forecasters, further cautioned by the visual evidence of thermometers outside apartment windows and the sound of the wind whipping beneath the eaves of old buildings, and the touch of the frigid blast that attacked any exploratory hand thrust outdoors for just an instant before a window slammed quickly shut again. They dressed with no regard to the dictates of fashion, the men wearing ear muffs and bulky mufflers, the women bundled into layers of sweaters and fur-lined boots, wearing woolen scarves to protect their heads and ears, rushing at a quick trot through the park, barely glancing at the bench or the black lunch pail sitting in the center of it. In a city notorious for its indifference, the citizens were more obviously withdrawn now, hurrying past each other without so much as eyes meeting, insulating themselves, becoming tight private cocoons that defied the cold. Speech might have made them more vulnerable, opening the mouth might have released the heat they had been storing up inside, commiseration would never help to diminish the wind that tried to cut them down in the streets, the saber-slash wind that blew in off the river and sent newspapers wildly soaring into the air, fedoras wheeling into the gutter. Speech was a precious commodity that cold March day.

In the park, Willis and Brown silently watched the bench.

The painters were in a garrulous mood.

"What have you got going, a stakeout?" the first painter asked.

"Is that what the walkie-talkie's for?" the second painter asked.

"Is there gonna be a bank holdup?"

"Is that why you're listening to that thing?"

"Shut up," Kling said encouragingly.

The painters were on their ladders, slopping apple green paint over everything in sight.

"We painted the D.A.'s office once," the first painter said.

"They were questioning this kid who stabbed his mother forty-seven times."

"Forty-*seven* times."

"In the belly, the head, the breasts, everyplace."

"With an icepick."

"He was guilty as sin."

"He said he did it to save her from the Martians."

"A regular bedbug."

"Forty-*seven* times."

"How could that save her from the Martians?" the second painter said.

"Maybe Martians don't like ladies with icepick holes in them," the first painter said, and burst out laughing. The second painter guffawed with him. Together, they perched on their ladders, helpless with laughter, limply holding brushes that dripped paint on the newspapers spread on the squadroom floor.

The man entered the park at ten A.M.

He was perhaps twenty-seven years old, with a narrow cold-pinched face, his lips drawn tight against the wind, his eyes watering. He wore a beige car coat, the collar pulled up against the back of his neck, buttoned tight around a green wool muffler at his throat. His hands were in the slash pockets of the coat. He wore brown corduroy trousers, the wale cut diagonally, and brown high-topped workman's shoes. He came onto the Clinton Street footpath swiftly, without looking either to the right or the left, walked immediately and directly to the third bench on the path, picked up the lunch pail, tucked it under his arm, put his naked hand back into his coat pocket, wheeled abruptly, and was starting out of the park again, when a voice behind him said, "Hold it right there, Mac."

He turned to see a tall burly Negro wearing what looked like a blue astronaut's suit. The Negro was holding a big pistol in his right hand. His left hand held a wallet which fell open to reveal a gold and blue shield.

"Police officer," the Negro said. "We want to talk to you."

Miranda-Escobedo sounds like a Mexican bull-fighter.

It is not.

It is the police shorthand for two separate Supreme Court decisions. These decisions, together, lay down the ground rules for the interrogation of suspects, and cops find them a supreme pain in the ass. There is not one working cop in the United States who thinks Miranda-Escobedo is a good idea. They are all fine Americans, these cops, and are all very concerned with the rights of the individual in a free society, but they do not like Miranda-Escobedo because they feel it makes their job more difficult. Their job is crime prevention.

Since the cops of the 87th had taken a suspect into custody and intended to question him, Miranda-Escobedo immediately came into play. Captain Frick, who was in charge of the entire precinct, had issued a bulletin to his men shortly after the Supreme Court decision in 1955, a flyer printed on green paper and advising every cop in the precinct, uniformed and plainclothes, on the proper interrogation of criminal suspects. Most of the precinct's uniformed cops carried the flyer clipped inside their notebooks where it was handy for reference whenever they needed it. The detectives, on the other hand, normally questioned more people than their uniformed colleagues, and had committed the rules to memory. They used them now with easy familiarity, while continuing to look upon them with great distaste.

"In keeping with the Supreme Court decision in *Miranda v. Arizona*," Hal Willis said, "we're required to advise you of your rights, and that's what I'm doing now. First, you have the right to remain silent if you choose, do you understand that?"

"I do."

"Do you also understand that you need not answer any police questions?"

"I do."

"And do you also understand that if you *do* answer questions, your answers may be used as evidence against you?"

"Yes, I understand."

"I must also inform you that you have the right to consult with an attorney before or during police questioning, do you understand that?"

"I understand."

"And if you decide to exercise that right but do not have the funds with which to hire counsel, you are entitled to have a lawyer appointed without cost, to consult with him before or during questioning. Is that clear?"

"Yes."

"You understand all of your rights as I have just explained them to you?"

"I do."

"Are you willing to answer questions without the presence of an attorney?"

"Gee, I don't know," the suspect said. "Should I?"

Willis and Brown looked at each other. They had thus far played Miranda-Escobedo by the book, warning the suspect of his privilege against self-incrimination, and warning him of his right to counsel. They had done so in explicit language, and not by merely making references to the Fifth Amendment. They had also made certain that the suspect understood his rights before asking him whether or not he wished to waive them. The green flyer issued by Captain Frick had warned that it was not sufficient for an officer simply to give the warnings and then proceed with an interrogation. It was necessary for the prisoner to *say* he understood, and that he was willing to answer questions without counsel. Only then would the court find that he had waived his constitutional rights.

In addition, however, the flyer had warned all police officers to exercise great care in avoiding language which could later be used by defense attorneys to charge that the officer had "threatened, tricked, or cajoled" the defendant into waiving. The officer was specifically cautioned against advising the suspect not to bother with a lawyer, or even implying that he'd be better off without a lawyer. He was, in short, supposed to inform the defendant of his privilege against self-incrimination and his right to counsel, period. Both Willis and Brown knew that they could not answer the suspect's question. If either of the two had advised him to answer questions without an attorney present, any confession they thereafter took would be inadmissible in court. If, on the other hand, they advised him *not* to answer questions, or advised him to consult with an attorney, their chances of getting a confession would be substantially lessened.

So Willis said, "I've explained your rights, and it would be improper for me to give you any advice. The decision is yours."

"Gee, I don't know," the man said.

"Well, think it over," Willis said.

The young man thought it over. Neither Willis nor Brown said a word. They knew that if their suspect refused to answer questions, that was it, the questioning would have to stop then and there. They also knew that if he began answering questions and suddenly decided he didn't want to go on with the interrogation, they would have to stop immediately, no matter what language he used to express his wishes—"I claim my rights," or "I don't want to say nothing else," or "I demand a mouthpiece."

So they waited.

"I got nothing to hide," the young man said at last.

"Are you willing to answer questions without the presence of an attorney?" Willis asked again.

"I am."

"What's your name?" Willis said.

"Anthony La Bresca."

"Where do you live, Anthony?"

"In Riverhead."

"Where in Riverhead, Anthony?" Brown said.

Both detectives had automatically fallen into the first-name basis of interrogation that violated only human dignity and not human rights, having nothing whatever to do with Miranda-Escobedo, but having everything in the world to do with the psychological unsettling of a prisoner. Call a man by his first name without allowing him the return courtesy and:

(a) You immediately make him a subordinate, and

(b) You instantly rob the familiarity of any friendly connotation, charging its use with menace instead.

"Where in Riverhead, Anthony?" Willis said.

"1812 Johnson."

"Live alone?"

"No, with my mother."

"Father dead?"

"They're separated."

"How old are you, Anthony?"

"Twenty-six."

"What do you do for a living?"

"I'm unemployed at the moment."

"What do you normally do?"

"I'm a construction worker."

"When was the last time you worked?"

"I was laid off last month."

"Why?"

"We completed the job."

"Haven't worked since?"

"I've been looking for work."

"But didn't have any luck, right?"

"That's right."

"Tell us about the lunch pail."

"What about it?"

"Well, what's *in* it, first of all?"

"Lunch, I guess," La Bresca said.

"Lunch, huh?"

"Isn't that what's usually in lunch pails?"

"We're asking *you*, Anthony."

"Yeah, lunch," La Bresca said.

"Did you call this squadroom yesterday?" Brown asked.

"No."

"How'd you know where that lunch pail would be?"

"I was told it would be there."

"Who told you?"

"This guy I met."

"What guy?"

"At the employment agency."

"Go on," Willis said, "let's hear it."

"I was waiting on line outside this employment agency on Ainsley, they handle a lot of construction jobs, you know, and that's where I got my last job from, so that's where I went back today. And this guy is standing on line with me, and all of a sudden he snaps his fingers and says, 'Jesus. I left my lunch in the park.' So I didn't say nothing, so he looks at me and says, 'How do you like that, I left my lunch on a park bench.' So I said that's a shame, and all, I sympathized with him, you know. What the hell, poor guy left his lunch on a park bench."

"So then what?"

"So he tells me he would run back into the park to get it, except he has a bum leg. So he asks me if I'd go get it for him."

"So naturally you said yes," Brown said. "A strange guy asks you to walk all the way from Ainsley Avenue over to Grover and into the park to pick up his lunch pail, so naturally you said yes."

"No, naturally I said no," La Bresca said.

"Then what were you doing in the park?"

"Well, we got to talking a little, and he explained how he got his leg hurt in World War II fighting against the Germans, picked up shrapnel from a mortar explosion, he had a pretty rough deal, you know?"

"So naturally you decided to go for the lunch pail after all."

"No, naturally I still didn't decide to do nothing."

"So how *did* you finally end up in the park?"

"That's what I've been trying to tell you."

"You took pity on this man, right? Because he had a bum leg, and because it was so cold outside, right?" Willis said.

"Well, yes and no."

"You didn't want him to have to walk all the way to the park, right?" Brown said.

"Well, yes and no. I mean, the guy was a stranger, why the hell should I care if he walked to the park or not?"

"Look, Anthony," Willis said, beginning to lose his temper, and trying to control himself, reminding himself that it was exceptionally difficult to interrogate suspects these days of Miranda-Escobedo when a man could simply refuse to answer at any given moment, Sorry, boys, no more questions, just shut your dear little flatfoot mouths or run the risk of blowing your case. "Look, Anthony," he said more gently, "we're only trying to find out how *you* happened to walk to the park and go directly to the third bench to pick up that lunch pail."

"I know," La Bresca said.

"You met a disabled war veteran, right?"

"Right."

"And he told you he left his lunch pail in the park."

"Well, he didn't say lunch *pail* at first. He just said *lunch*."

"When did he say lunch *pail*?"

"After he gave me the five bucks."

"Oh, he offered you five dollars to go get his lunch pail, is that it?"

"He didn't offer it to me, he *handed* it to me."

"He handed you five bucks and said, 'Would you go get my lunch pail for me?'"

"That's right. And he told me it would be on the third bench in the park, on the Clinton Street footpath. Which is right where it was."

"What were you supposed to do with this lunch pail after you got it?"

"Bring it back to him. He was holding my place in line."

"Mm-huh," Brown said.

"What's so important about that lunch pail, anyway?" La Bresca asked.

"Nothing," Willis said. "Tell us about this man. What did he look like?"

"Ordinary-looking guy."

"How old would you say he was?"

"Middle thirties, thirty-five, something like that."

"Tall, short, or average?"

"Tall. About six feet, I would say, give or take."

"What about his build? Heavy, medium, or slight?"

"He was built nice. Good shoulders."

"Heavy?"

"Husky, I would say. A good build."

"What color was his hair?"

"Blond."

"Was he wearing a mustache or a beard?"

"No."

"What color were his eyes, did you notice?"

"Blue."

"Did you notice any scars or identifying marks?"

"No."

"Tattoos?"

"No."

"What sort of voice did he have?"

"Average voice. Not too deep. Just average. A good voice."

"Any accent or regional dialect?"

"No."

"What was he wearing?"

"Brown overcoat, brown gloves."

"Suit?"

"I couldn't see what he had on under the coat. I mean, he was wearing pants, naturally, but I didn't notice what color they were, and I couldn't tell you whether they were part of a suit or whether . . ."

"Fine, was he wearing a hat?"

"No hat."

"Glasses."

"No glasses."

"Anything else you might have noticed about him?"

"Yeah," La Bresca said.

"What?"

"He was wearing a hearing aid."

The employment agency was on the corner of Ainsley Avenue and Clinton Street, five blocks north of the entrance to the park's Clinton Street footpath. On the off chance that the man wearing the hearing aid would still be waiting for La Bresca's return, they checked out a sedan and drove from the station house. La Bresca sat in the back of the car, willing and eager to identify the man if he was still there.

There was a line of men stretching halfway around the corner of Clinton, burly men in work clothes and caps, hands thrust into coat pockets, faces white with cold, feet moving incessantly as they shuffled and jigged and tried to keep warm.

"You'd think they were giving away dollar bills up there," La Bresca said. "Actually, they charge you a whole week's pay. They got good jobs, though. The last one they got me paid real good, and it lasted eight months."

"Do you see your man anywhere on that line?" Brown asked.

"I can't tell from here. Can we get out?"

"Yeah, sure," Brown said.

They parked the car at the curb. Willis, who had been driving, got out first. He was small and light, with the easy grace of a dancer and the steady cold gaze of a blackjack dealer. He kept slapping his gloved hands together as he waited for Brown. Brown came out of the car like a rhinoceros, pushing his huge body through the door frame, slamming the door behind him, and then pulling his gloves on over big-knuckled hands.

"Did you throw the visor?" Willis asked.

"No. We'll only be a minute here."

"You'd better throw it. Goddamn eager beavers'll give us a ticket sure as hell."

Brown grunted and went back into the car.

"Boy, it's cold out here," La Bresca said.

"Yeah," Willis said.

In the car, Brown lowered the sun visor. A hand-lettered cardboard sign was fastened to the visor with rubber bands. It read:

POLICE DEPARTMENT VEHICLE

The car door slammed again. Brown came over and nodded, and together, they began walking toward the line of men standing on the sidewalk. Both detectives unbuttoned their overcoats.

"Do you see him?" Brown asked La Bresca.

"Not yet," La Bresca said.

They walked the length of the line slowly.

"Well?" Brown asked.

"No," La Bresca said. "He ain't here."

"Let's take a look upstairs," Willis suggested.

The line of job seekers continued up a flight of rickety wooden steps to a dingy second-floor office. The lettering on a frosted glass door read:

MERIDIAN EMPLOYMENT AGENCY

JOBS OUR SPECIALTY

"See him?" Willis asked.

"No," La Bresca said.

"Wait here," Willis said, and the two detectives moved away from him, toward the other end of the corridor.

"What do you think?" Brown asked.

"What can we hold him on?"

"Nothing."

"So *that's* what I think."

"Is he worth a tail?"

"It depends on how serious the loot thinks this is."

"Why don't you ask him?"

"I think I will. Hold the fort."

Brown went back to La Bresca. Willis found a pay phone around the bend in the corridor, and dialed the squadroom. The lieutenant listened carefully to everything he had to report, and then said, "How do you read him?"

"I think he's telling the truth."

"You think there really *was* some guy with a hearing aid?"

"Yes."

"Then why'd he leave before La Bresca got back with the pail?"

"I don't know, Pete. I just don't make La Bresca for a thief."

"Where'd you say he lived?"

"1812 Johnson. In Riverhead."

"What precinct would that be?"

"I don't know."

"I'll check it out and give them a ring. Maybe they can spare a man for a tail. Christ knows we can't."

"So shall we turn La Bresca loose?"

"Yeah, come on back here. Give him a little scare first, though, just in case."

"Right," Willis said, and hung up, and went back to where La Bresca and Brown were waiting.

"Okay, Anthony," Willis said, "you can go."

"Go? Who's *going* anyplace? I got to get back on that line again. I'm trying to get a job here."

"And remember, Anthony, if anything happens, we know where to find you."

"What do you mean? What's gonna happen?"

"Just remember."

"Sure," La Bresca said. He paused and then said, "Listen, you want to do me a favor?"

"What's that?"

"Get me up to the front of the line there."

"How can we do that?"

"Well, you're cops, ain't you?" La Bresca asked, and Willis and Brown looked at each other.

When they got back to the squadroom, they learned that Lieutenant Byrnes had called the 115th in Riverhead and had been informed they could not spare a man for the surveillance of Anthony La Bresca. Nobody seemed terribly surprised.

That night, as Parks Commissioner Cowper came down the broad white marble steps outside Philharmonic Hall, his wife clinging to his left arm, swathed in mink and wearing a diaphanous white scarf on her head, the commissioner himself resplendent in black tie and dinner jacket, the mayor and his wife four steps ahead, the sky virtually starless, a bitter brittle dryness to the air, that night as the parks commissioner came down the steps of Philharmonic Hall with the huge two-story-high windows behind him casting warm yellow light onto the windswept steps and pavement, that night as the commissioner lifted his left foot preparatory to placing it on the step below, laughing at something his wife said in his ear, his laughter billowing out of his mouth in puffs of visible vapor that whipped away on the wind like comic strip balloons, that night as he tugged on his right-hand glove with his already gloved left hand, that night two shots cracked into the plaza, shattering the wintry stillness, and the commissioner's laugh stopped, the commissioner's hand stopped, the commissioner's foot stopped, and he tumbled headlong down the steps, blood pouring from his forehead and his cheek, and his wife screamed, and the mayor turned to see what was the matter, and an enterprising photographer on the sidewalk caught the toppling commissioner on film for posterity.

He was dead long before his body rolled to a stop on the wide white bottom step.

3

CONCETTA ESPOSITA LA BRESCA HAD BEEN TAUGHT ONLY to dislike and distrust all Negroes. Her brothers, on the other hand, had been taught to dismember them if possible. They had learned their respective lessons in a sprawling slum ghetto affectionately and sarcastically dubbed Paradiso by its largely Italian population. Concetta, as a growing child in this dubious garden spot, had watched her brothers and other neighborhood boys bash in a good many Negro skulls when she was still just a *piccola ragazza*. The mayhem did not disturb her. Concetta figured if you were stupid enough to be born a Negro, and were further stupid enough to come wandering into Paradiso, why then you deserved to have your fool black head split wide open every now and then.

Concetta had left Paradiso at the age of nineteen, when the local iceman, a fellow *Napolitano* named

Carmine La Bresca, moved his business to Riverhead and asked the youngest of the Esposito girls to marry him. She readily accepted because he was a handsome fellow with deep brown eyes and curly black hair, and because he had a thriving business of which he was the sole owner. She also accepted because she was pregnant at the time.

Her son was born seven months later, and he was now twenty-seven years old, and living alone with Concetta in the second-floor apartment of a two-family house on Johnson Street. Carmine La Bresca had gone back to Pozzuoli, fifteen miles outside of Naples, a month after Anthony was born. The last Concetta heard of him was a rumor that he had been killed during World War II, but, knowing her husband, she suspected he was king of the icemen somewhere in Italy, still fooling around with young girls and getting them pregnant in the icehouse, as was her own cruel misfortune.

Concetta Esposita La Bresca still disliked and distrusted all Negroes, and she was rather startled—to say the least—to find one on her doorstep at 12:01 A.M. on a starless, moonless night.

"What is it?" she shouted. "Go away."

"Police officer," Brown said, and flashed the tin, and it was then that Concetta noticed the other man standing with the Negro, a white man, short, with a narrow face and piercing brown eyes, *madonna mia*, it looked as if he was giving her the *malocchio*.

"What do you want, go away," she said in a rush, and lowered the shade on the glass-paneled rear door of her apartment. The door was at the top of a rickety flight of wooden steps (Willis had almost tripped and broken his neck on the third one from the top) overlooking a back yard in which there was a tar-paper-covered tree. (Doubtless a fig tree, Brown remarked on their way up the steps.) A clothesline stiff with undergarments stretched from the tiny back porch outside the glass-paneled door to a pole set diagonally at the other end of the yard. The wind whistled around the porch and did its best to blow Willis off and down into the grape arbor covering the outside patio below. He knocked on the door again, and shouted, "Police officers, you'd better open up, lady."

"Sta zitto!" Concetta said, and unlocked the door. "You want to wake the whole neighbor? *Ma che vergogna!"*

"Is it all right to come in, lady?" Willis asked.

"Come in, come in," Concetta said, and stepped back into the small kitchen, allowing Willis and then Brown to pass her.

"So what you want two o'clock in the morning?" Concetta said, and closed the door against the wind. The kitchen was narrow, the stove, sink, and refrigerator lined up against one wall, an enamel-topped table on the opposite wall. A metal cabinet, its door open to reveal an array of breakfast cereals and canned foods, was on the right-angled wall, alongside a radiator. There was a mirror over the sink and a porcelain dog on top of the refrigerator. Hanging on the wall over the radiator was a picture of Jesus Christ. A light bulb with a pull chain and a large glass globe hung in the center of the kitchen. The faucet was dripping. An electric clock over the range hummed a steady counterpoint.

"It's only midnight," Brown said. "Not two o'clock."

There was an edge to his voice that had not been there on the long ride up to Riverhead, and Willis could only attribute it to the presence of Mrs. La Bresca, if indeed that was who the lady was. He wondered for perhaps the hundredth time what radar Brown possessed that enabled him to pinpoint unerringly any bigot within a radius of thousand yards. The woman was staring at both men with equal animosity, it seemed to Willis, her long black hair pinned into a bun at the back of her head, her brown eyes slitted and defiant. She was wearing a man's bathrobe over her nightgown, and he saw now that she was barefoot.

"Are you Mrs. La Bresca?" Willis asked.

"I am Concetta La Bresca, who wants to know?" she said.

"Detectives Willis and Brown of the 87th Squad," Willis said. "Where's your son?"

"He's asleep," Concetta said, and because she was born in Naples and raised in Paradiso, immediately assumed it was necessary to provide him with an alibi. "He was here with me all night," she said, "you got the wrong man."

"You want to wake him up, Mrs. La Bresca?" Brown said.

"What for?"

"We'd like to talk to him."

"What for?"

"Ma'am, we can take him into custody, if that's what you'd like," Brown said, "but it might be easier all around if we just asked him a few simple questions right here and now. You want to go fetch him, ma'am?"

"I'm up," La Bresca's voice said from the other room.

"You want to come out here, please, Mr. La Bresca?" Willis said.

"He was here all night," Concetta said, but Brown's hand drifted nonetheless toward the revolver holstered at his waist, just in case La Bresca had been out pumping two bullets into the commissioner's head instead. He was a while coming. When he finally opened the door and walked into the kitchen, he was carrying nothing more lethal in his hand than the sash of his bathrobe, which he knotted about his waist. His hair was tousled, and his eyes were bleary.

"What now?" he asked.

Since this was a field investigation, and since La Bresca couldn't conceivably be considered "in custody," neither Willis nor Brown felt it necessary to advise him of his rights. Instead, Willis immediately said, "Where were you tonight at eleven-thirty?"

"Right here," La Bresca said.

"Doing what?"

"Sleeping."

"What time'd you go to bed?"

"About ten."

"You always hit the sack so early?"

"I do when I gotta get up early."

"You getting up early tomorrow?"

"Six A.M.," La Bresca said.

"Why?"

"To get to work."

"We thought you were unemployed."

"I got a job this afternoon, right after you guys left me."

"What kind of a job?"

"Construction work. I'm a laborer."

"Meridian get you the job?"

"That's right."

"Who with?"

"Erhard Engineering."

"In Riverhead?"

"No, Isola."

"What time'd you get home tonight?" Brown asked.

"I left Meridian, it musta been about one o'clock, I guess. I went up the pool hall on South Leary and shot a few games with the boys. Then I came home here, it musta been about five or six o'clock."

"What'd you do then?"

"He ate," Concetta said.

"Then what?"

"I watched a little TV, and got into bed," La Bresca said.

"Can anybody besides your mother verify that story?"

"Nobody was here, if that's what you mean."

"You get any phone calls during the night?"

"No."

"Just your word then, right?"

"And *mine*," Concetta said.

"Listen, I don't know what you guys want from me," La Bresca said. "But I'm telling you the truth, I mean it. What's going on, anyway?"

"Did you happen to catch the news on television?"

"No, I musta fell asleep before the news went on. Why? What happened?"

"I go in his room and turn off the light at ten-thirty," Concetta said.

"I wish you guys would believe me," La Bresca said. "Whatever it is you've got in mind, I didn't have nothing to do with it."

"I believe you," Willis said. "How about you, Artie?"

"I believe him, too," Brown said.

"But we have to ask questions," Willis said, "you understand?"

"Sure, I understand," La Bresca said, "but I mean, it's the middle of the night, you know? I gotta get up tomorrow morning."

"Why don't you tell us about the man with the hearing aid again," Willis suggested gently.

They spent at least another fifteen minutes questioning La Bresca and at the end of that time decided they'd either have to pull him in and charge him with something, or else forget him for the time being. The man who'd called the squadroom had said, "There are more than one of us," and his information had been passed from Kling to the other detectives on the squad, and it was only this nagging knowledge that kept them there questioning La Bresca long after they should have stopped. A cop can usually tell whether he's onto real meat or not, and La Bresca did not seem like a thief. Willis had told the lieutenant just that only this afternoon, and his opinion hadn't changed in the intervening hours. But if there *was* a gang involved in the commissioner's murder, wasn't it possible that La Bresca was one of them? A lowly cog in the organization, perhaps, the gopher, the slob who was sent to pick up things, the expendable man who ran the risk of being caught by the police if anything went wrong? In which case, La Bresca was lying.

Well, if he was lying, he did it like an expert, staring out of his baby blues and melting both those hardhearted cops with tales of the new job he was anxious to start tomorrow morning, which is why he'd gone to bed so early and all, got to get a full eight hours' sleep, growing mind in a growing body, red-blooded second-generation American, and all that crap. Which raised yet another possibility. If he *was* lying—and so far they hadn't been able to trip him up, hadn't been able to budge him from his description of the mystery man he'd met outside Meridian, hadn't been able to find a single discrepancy between the story he'd told that afternoon and the one he was telling now—but if he *was* lying, then wasn't it possible the caller and La Bresca were one and the same person? *Not* a gang at all, that being a figment of his own imagination, a tiny falsehood designed to lead the police into believing this was a well-organized group instead of a single ambitious hood trying to make a killing. And if La Bresca and the caller were one and the same, then La Bresca and the man who'd murdered the commissioner were also one and the same. In which case, it would be proper to take the little liar home and book him for murder. Sure, and then try to find something that would stick, *anything* that would stick, they'd be laughed out of court right at the preliminary hearing.

Some nights you can't make a nickel.

So after fifteen minutes of some very fancy footwork
designed to befuddle and unsettle La Bresca, with
Brown utilizing his very special logically persistent
method of questioning while Willis sniped and jabbed
around the edges, they knew nothing more than they had
known that afternoon. The only difference was that now
the commissioner was dead. So they thanked Mrs. La
Bresca for the use of the hall, and they shook hands with
her son and apologized for having pulled him out of bed,
and they wished him luck at his new job, and then they
both said good night again and went out of the house and
heard Mrs. La Bresca locking the kitchen door behind
them, and went down the rickety wooden steps, and
down the potholed driveway, and across the street to
where they had parked the police sedan.

Then Willis started the car, and turned on the heater,
and both men talked earnestly and softly for several mo-
ments and decided to ask the lieutenant for permission to
bug La Bresca's phone in the morning.

Then they went home.

It was cold and dark in the alley where Steve Carella
lay on his side huddled in a tattered overcoat. The late
February snow had been shoveled and banked against
one brick alley wall, soiled now with the city's grime, a
thin layer of soot crusted onto its surface. Carella was
wearing two pairs of thermal underwear and a quilted
vest. In addition, a hand warmer was tucked into one
pocket of the vest, providing a good steady heat inside
the threadbare overcoat. But he was cold.

The banked snow opposite him only made him

colder. He did not like snow. Oh yes, he could remember
owning his own sled as a boy, and he could remember
belly-whopping with joyous abandon, but the memory
seemed like a totally fabricated one in view of his
present very real aversion to snow. Snow was cold and
wet. If you were a private citizen, you had to shovel it,
and if you were a Department of Sanitation worker, you
had to truck it over to the River Dix to get rid of it. Snow
was a pain in the ass.

This entire stakeout was a pain in the ass.

But it was also very amusing.

It was the amusing part of it that kept Carella lying in
a cold dark alley on a night that wasn't fit for man or
beast. (Of course, he had also been *ordered* to lie in a
cold dark alley by the lieutenant for whom he worked,
nice fellow name of Peter Byrnes, *he* should come lie in
a cold dark alley some night.) The amusing part of this
particular stakeout was that Carella wasn't planted in a
bank hoping to prevent a multimillion dollar robbery,
nor was he planted in a candy store someplace, hoping
to crack an international ring of narcotics peddlers, nor
was he even hidden in the bathroom of a spinster lady's
apartment, hoping to catch a mad rapist. He was lying in
a cold dark alley, and the amusing part was that two vagrants had been set on fire. That wasn't so amusing, the
part about being set on fire. That was pretty serious. The
amusing part was that the victims had been vagrants. Ever
since Carella could remember, the police had been
waging an unremitting war against this city's vagrants,
arresting them, jailing them, releasing them, arresting
them again, on and on ad infinitum. So now the police had
been presented with two benefactors who were gener-

ously attempting to rid the streets of any and all bums by setting them aflame, and what did the police do? The police promptly dispatched a valuable man to a cold dark alley to lie on his side facing a dirty snowbank while hoping to catch the very fellows who were in charge of incinerating bums. It did not make sense. It was amusing.

A lot of things about police work were amusing.

It was certainly funnier to be lying here freezing than to be at home in bed with a warm and loving woman; oh God, that was so amusing it made Carella want to weep. He thought of Teddy alone in bed, black hair spilling all over the pillow, half-smile on her mouth, nylon gown pulled back over curving hip, God, I could freeze to death right here in this goddamn alley, he thought, and my own wife won't learn about it till morning. My own passionate wife! She'll read about it in the papers! She'll see my name on page four! She'll—

There were footsteps at the other end of the alley.

He felt himself tensing. Beneath the overcoat, his naked hand moved away from the warmer and dropped swiftly to the cold steel butt of his service revolver. He eased the gun out of its holster, lay hunched on his side with the gun ready, and waited as the footsteps came closer.

"Here's one," a voice.

It was a young voice.

"Yeah," another voice answered.

Carella waited. His eyes were closed, he lay huddled in the far corner of the alley, simulating sleep, his finger curled inside the trigger guard now, a hair's-breadth away from the trigger itself.

Somebody kicked him.

"Wake up!" a voice said.

He moved swiftly, but not swiftly enough. He was shoving himself off the floor of the alley, yanking the revolver into firing position, when the liquid splashed onto the front of his coat.

"Have a drink!" one of the boys shouted, and Carella saw a match flare into life, and suddenly he was in flames.

His reaction sequence was curious in that his sense of smell supplied the first signal, the unmistakable aroma of gasoline fumes rising from the front of his coat, and then the flaring match, shocking in itself, providing a brilliant tiny explosion of light in the nearly black alley, more shocking in combination with the smell of the gasoline. Warning slammed with physical force into his temples, streaked in a jagged electric path to the back of his skull, and suddenly there were flames. There was no shock coupled with the fire that leaped up toward his face from the front of his coat. There was only terror.

Steve Carella reacted in much the same way Cro-Magnon must have reacted the first time he ventured too close to a raging fire and discovered that flames can cook people as well as saber-toothed tigers. He dropped his weapon, he covered his face, he whirled abruptly, instinctively rushing for the soot-crusted snowbank across the alley, forgetting his attackers, only vaguely aware that they were running, laughing, out of the alley and into the night, thinking only in a jagged broken pattern fire run burn fire out fire fire and hurling himself full length onto the snow. His hands were cupped tightly to his face, he could feel the flames chewing angrily at the backs of them, could smell the terrifying stench of burning hair and flesh, and then heard the sizzle of fire in contact with the snow, felt the cold and comforting snow, was suddenly enveloped in a white cloud of steam that rose from the beautiful snow, rolled from shoulder to shoulder in the glorious marvelous soothing beneficial white and magnificent snow, and found tears in his eyes, and thought nothing, and lay with his face pressed to the snow for a long while, breathing heavily, and still thinking nothing.

He got up at last and painfully retrieved his discarded revolver and walked slowly to the mouth of the alley and looked at his hands in the light of the street lamp. He caught his breath, and then went to the call box on the next corner. He told Sergeant Murchison at the desk that the fire bugs had hit, and that his hands had been burned and he would need a meat wagon to get him over to the hospital. Murchison said, "Are you all right?" and Carella looked at his hands again, and said, "Yes, I'm all right, Dave."

4

Detective Bert Kling was in love, but nobody else was.

The mayor was not in love, he was furious. The mayor called the police commissioner in high dudgeon and wanted to know what kind of a goddamn city this was where a man of the caliber of Parks Commissioner Cowper could be gunned down on the steps of Philharmonic Hall, what the hell kind of a city was this, anyway?

"Well, sir," the police commissioner started, but the mayor said, "Perhaps you can tell me why adequate police protection was not provided for Commissioner Cowper when his wife informs me this morning that the police *knew* a threat had been made on his life, perhaps you can tell me that," the mayor shouted into the phone.

"Well, sir," the police commissioner started, but the

mayor said, "Or perhaps you can tell me why you still haven't located the apartment from which those shots were fired, when the autopsy has already revealed the angle of entrance and your ballistics people have come up with a probable trajectory, perhaps you can tell me that."

"Well, sir," the police commissioner started, but the mayor said, "Get me some results, do you want this city to become a laughingstock?"

The police commissioner certainly didn't want the city to become a laughingstock, so he said, "Yes, sir, I'll do the best I can," and the mayor said, "You had better," and hung up.

There was no love lost between the mayor and the police commissioner that morning. So the police commissioner asked his secretary, a tall wan blond man who appeared consumptive and who claimed his constant hacking cough was caused by smoking three packs of cigarettes a day in a job that was enough to drive anyone utterly mad, the police commissioner asked his secretary to find out what the mayor had meant by a threat on the parks commissioner's life, and report back to him immediately. The tall wan blond secretary got to work at once, asking around here and there, and discovering that the 87th Precinct had indeed logged several telephone calls from a mysterious stranger who had threatened to kill the parks commissioner unless five thousand dollars was delivered to him by noon yesterday. When the police commissioner received this information, he said, "Oh, *yeah*?" and immediately dialed Frederick 7-8024, and asked to talk to Detective-Lieutenant Peter Byrnes.

Detective-Lieutenant Peter Byrnes had enough headaches that morning, what with Carella in the hospital with second-degree burns on the backs of both hands, and the painters having moved from the squadroom into his own private office, where they were slopping up everything in sight and telling jokes on their ladders. Byrnes was not overly fond of the police commissioner to begin with, the commissioner being a fellow who had been imported from a neighboring city when the new administration took over, a city which, in Byrnes' opinion, had an even larger crime rate than this one. Nor was the new commissioner terribly fond of Lieutenant Byrnes, because Byrnes was the sort of garrulous Irishman who shot off his mouth at Police Benevolent Association and Emerald Society functions, letting anyone within earshot know what he thought of the mayor's recent whiz-kid appointee. So there was hardly any sweetness and light oozing over the telephone wires that morning between the commissioner's office at headquarters downtown on High Street, and Byrnes' paint-spattered corner office on the second floor of the grimy station house on Grover Avenue.

"What's this all about, Byrnes?" the commissioner asked.

"Well, sir," Byrnes said, remembering that the *former* commissioner used to call him Pete, "we received several threatening telephone calls from an unidentified man yesterday, which telephone calls I discussed personally with Parks Commissioner Cowper."

"What did you do about those calls, Byrnes?"

"We placed the drop site under surveillance, and apprehended the man who made the pickup."

"So what happened?"

"We questioned him and released him."

"Why?"

"Insufficient evidence. He was also interrogated after the parks commissioner's murder last night. We did not have ample grounds for an arrest. The man is still free, but a telephone tap went into effect this morning, and we're ready to move in if we monitor anything incriminating."

"Why wasn't the commissioner given police protection?"

"I offered it, sir, and it was refused."

"Why wasn't your suspect put under surveillance *before* a crime was committed?"

"I couldn't spare any men, sir, and when I contacted the 115th in Riverhead, where the suspect resides, I was told they could not spare any men either. Besides, as I told you, the commissioner did not *want* protection. He felt we were dealing with a crackpot, sir, and I must tell you that was our opinion here, too. Until, of course, recent events proved otherwise."

"Why hasn't that apartment been found yet?"

"What apartment, sir?"

"The apartment from which the two shots were fired that killed Parks Commissioner Cowper."

"Sir, the crime was not committed in our precinct. Philharmonic Hall, sir, is in the 53rd Precinct and, as I'm sure the commissioner realizes, a homicide is investigated by the detectives assigned to the squad in the precinct in which the homicide was committed."

"Don't give me any of that bullshit, Byrnes," the police commissioner said.

"That is the way we do it in this city, sir," Byrnes said.

"This is your case," the commissioner answered. "You got that, Byrnes?"

"If you say so, sir."

"I say so. Get some men over to the area, and find that goddamn apartment."

"Yes, sir."

"And report back to me."

"Yes, sir," Byrnes said, and hung up.

"Getting a little static, huh?" the first painter said.

"Getting your ass chewed out, huh?" the second painter said.

Both men were on their ladders, grinning and dripping apple green paint on the floor.

"Get the hell out of this office!" Byrnes shouted.

"We ain't finished yet," the first painter said.

"We don't leave till we finish," the second painter said.

"That's our orders," the first painter said.

"We don't work for the Police Department, you know."

"We work for the Department of Public Works."

"Maintenance and Repair."

"And we don't quit a job till we finish it."

"Stop dripping paint all over my goddamn floor!" Byrnes shouted, and stormed out of the office. "Hawes!" he shouted. "Kling! Willis! Brown! Where the hell *is* everybody?" he shouted.

Meyer came out of the men's room, zipping up his fly. "What's up, Skipper?" he said.

"Where were you?"

"Taking a leak. Why, what's up?"

"Get somebody over to the area!" Byrnes shouted.

"What area?"

"Where the goddamn commissioner got shot!"

"Okay, sure," Meyer said. "But why? That's not our case."

"It is now."

"Oh?"

"Who's catching?"

"I am."

"Where's Kling?"

"Day off."

"Where's Brown?"

"On that wire tap."

"And Willis?"

"He went to the hospital to see Steve."

"And Hawes?"

"He went down for some Danish."

"What the hell am I running here, a resort in the mountains?"

"No, sir. We . . ."

"Send Hawes over there! Send him over the minute he gets back. Get on the phone to Ballistics. Find out what they've got. Call the M.E.'s office and get that autopsy report. Get cracking, Meyer!"

"Yes, *sir!*" Meyer snapped, and went immediately to the telephone.

"This goddamn racket drives me crazy," Byrnes said, and started to storm back into his office, remembered that the jolly green painters were in there slopping around, and stormed into the Clerical Office instead.

"Get those files in order!" he shouted. "What the hell do you do in here all day, Miscolo, make coffee?"

"Sir?" Miscolo said, because that's exactly what he was doing at the moment.

Bert Kling was in love.

It was not a good time of the year to be in love. It is better to be in love when flowers are blooming and balmy breezes are wafting in off the river, and strange animals come up to lick your hand. There's only one good thing about being in love in March, and that's that it's better to be in love in March than not to be in love at all, as the wise man once remarked.

Bert Kling was madly in love.

He was madly in love with a girl who was twenty-three years old, full-breasted and wide-hipped, her blond hair long and trailing midway down her back or sometimes curled into a honey conch shell at the back of her head, her eyes a cornflower blue, a tall girl who came just level with his chin when she was wearing heels. He was madly in love with a scholarly girl who was studying at night for her master's degree in psychology while working during the day conducting interviews for a firm downtown on Shepherd Street; a serious girl who hoped to go on for her Ph.D., and then pass the state boards, and then practice psychology; a nutty girl who was capable of sending to the squadroom a six-foot high heart cut out of plywood and painted red and lettered in yellow with the words Cynthia Forrest Loves Detective 3rd/Grade Bertram Kling, So Is That A Crime?, as she had done on St. Valentine's Day just last month (and which Kling had still not heard the end of from all his comical colleagues); an emotional girl who could burst into tears at the sight of a blind man playing an accordian on The Stem, to whom she gave a five-dollar bill, merely put the bill silently into the cup, soundlessly, it did not even make a rustle, and turned away to weep into Kling's shoulder; a passionate girl who clung to him fiercely in the night and who woke him sometimes at six in the morning to say, "Hey, Cop, I have to go to work in a few hours, are you interested?" to which Kling invariably answered, "No, I am not interested in sex and things like that," and then kissed her until she was dizzy and afterwards sat across from her at the kitchen table in her apartment, staring at her, marveling at her beauty and once caused her to blush when he said, "There's a woman who sells *pidaguas* on Mason Avenue, her name is Illuminada, she was born in Puerto Rico. Your name should be Illuminada, Cindy. You fill the room with light."

Boy, was he in love.

But, it being March, and the streets still banked high with February snow, and the winds howling, and the wolves growling and chasing civilians in troikas who cracked whips and huddled in bear rugs, it being a bitter cold winter which seemed to have started in September and showed no signs of abating till next August, when possibly, but just possibly, all the snow might melt and the flowers would bloom—it being that kind of a treacherous winter, what better to do than discuss police work? What better to do than rush along the frozen street on Cindy's lunch hour with her hand clutched tightly in the crook of his arm and the wind whipping around them and drowning out Kling's voice as he tried to tell her of the mysterious circumstances surrounding the death of Parks Commissioner Cowper.

"Yes, it *sounds* very mysterious," Cindy said, and brought her hand out of her pocket in an attempt to keep the wind from tearing the kerchief from her head. "Listen, Bert," she said, "I'm really very tired of winter, aren't you tired of it?"

"Yeah," Kling said. "Listen, Cindy, you know who I hope this isn't?"

"Hope who isn't?" she said.

"The guy who made the calls. The guy who killed the commissioner. You know who I hope we're not up against?"

"Who?" she asked.

"The deaf man," he said.

"What?" she said.

"He was a guy we went up against a few years back, it must have been maybe seven, eight years ago. He tore this whole damn city apart trying to rob a bank. He was the smartest crook we ever came up against."

"*Who?*" Cindy said.

"The deaf man," Kling said again.

"Yes, but what's his name?"

"We don't know his name. We never caught him. He jumped in the river and we thought he drowned, but maybe he's back now. Like Frankenstein."

"Like Frankenstein's monster, you mean," Cindy said.

"Yeah, like him. Remember he was supposed to have died in that fire, but he didn't."

"I remember."

"That was a scary picture," Kling said.

"I wet my pants when I saw it," Cindy said. "And that was on television."

"You wet your pants on *television?*" Kling said. "In front of forty million *people?*"

"No, I saw *Frankenstein* on television," Cindy said, and grinned and poked him.

"The deaf man," Kling said. "I hope it's not him."

It was the first time any man on the squad had voiced the possibility that the commissioner's murderer was the man who had given them so much trouble so many years ago. The thought was somewhat numbing. Bert Kling was a young man, and not a particularly philosophical one, but he intuitively understood that the deaf man (who had once signed a note L. Sordo, very comical, El Sordo meaning "The Deaf One" in Spanish) was capable of manipulating odds with computer accuracy, of spreading confusion and fear, of juggling permutations and combinations in a manner calculated to upset the strict and somewhat bureaucratic efficiency of a police precinct, making law enforcers behave like bumbling Keystone cops in a yellowing ancient film, knew instinctively and with certainty that if the commissioner's murderer was indeed the deaf man, they had not yet heard the end of all this. And because the very thought of what the deaf man might and *could* do was too staggering to contemplate, Kling involuntarily shuddered, and he knew it was not from the cold.

"I hope it isn't him," he said, and his words were carried away on the wind.

"Kiss me," Cindy said suddenly, "and then buy me a hot chocolate, you cheapskate."

The boy who came into the muster room that Wednesday afternoon was about twelve years old.

He was wearing his older brother's hand-me-down ski parka which was blue and three sizes too large for him. He had pulled the hood of the parka up over his head, and had tightened the drawstrings around his neck, but the hood was still too big, and it kept falling off. He kept trying to pull it back over his head as he came into the station house carrying an envelope in the same hand with which he wiped his runny nose. He was wearing high-topped sneakers with the authority of all slum kids who wear sneakers winter and summer, all year round, despite the warnings of podiatrists. He walked to the muster desk with a sneaker-inspired bounce, tried to adjust the parka hood again, wiped his dripping nose again, and then looked up at Sergeant Murchison and said, "You the desk sergeant?"

"I'm the desk sergeant," Murchison answered without looking up from the absentee slips he was filling out from that morning's muster sheet. It was 2:10 P.M., and in an hour and thirty-five minutes the afternoon shift of uniformed cops would be coming in, and there'd be a new roll call to take, and new absentee slips to fill out, a regular rat race, he should have become a fireman or a postman.

"I'm supposed to give you this," the kid said, and reached up to hand Murchison the sealed envelope.

"Thanks," Murchison said, and accepted the envelope without looking at the kid, and then suddenly raised his head and said, "Hold it just a second."

"Why, what's the matter?"

"Just hold it right there a second," Murchison said, and opened the envelope. He unfolded the single sheet of white paper that been neatly folded in three equal parts, and he read what was on the sheet, and then he looked down at the kid again and said, "Where'd you get this?"

"Outside."

"Where?"

"A guy gave it to me."

"What guy?"

"A tall guy outside."

"Outside where?"

"Near the park there. Across the street."

"Gave you this?"

"Yeah."

"What'd he say?"

"Said I should bring it in here and give it to the desk sergeant."

"You know the guy?"

"No, he gave me five bucks to bring it over here."

"What'd he look like?"

"A tall guy with blond hair. He had a thing in his ear."

"What kind of a thing?"

"Like he was deaf," the kid said, and wiped his hand across his nose again.

That was what the note read.

So they studied the note, being careful not to get any more fingerprints on it than Sergeant Murchison had already put there, and then they stood around a runny-nosed twelve-year-old-kid wearing a blue ski parka three sizes too large for him, and fired questions at him as though they had captured Jack the Ripper over from London for the weekend.

They got nothing from the kid except perhaps his cold.

He repeated essentially what he had told Sergeant Murchison, that a tall blond guy wearing a thing in his ear (A hearing aid, you mean, kid?) yeah, a thing in his ear, had stopped him across the street from the police station and offered him five bucks to carry an envelope in to the desk sergeant. The kid couldn't see nothing wrong with bringing an envelope into the police station, so he done it, and that was all, he didn't even know who the guy with the thing in his ear was. (You mean a hearing aid kid?) Yeah, a thing in his ear, he didn't know who he was, never even seen him around the neighborhood or nothing, so could he go home now because he had to make a stop at Linda's Boutique to pick up some dresses for his sister who did sewing at home for Mrs. Montana? (He was wearing a hearing aid, huh, kid?) Yeah, a thing in his ear, the kid said.

So they let the kid go at two-thirty without even offering him an ice cream cone or some gumdrops, and then they sat around the squadroom handling the suspect note with a pair of tweezers and decided to send it over to Lieutenant Sam Grossman at the police lab in the hope that he could lift some latent prints that did not belong to Sergeant Murchison.

None of them mentioned the deaf man.

Nobody likes to talk about ghosts.

Or even *think* about them.

"Hello, Bernice," Meyer said into the telephone, "is your boss around? Yeah, sure, I'll wait."

Patiently, he tapped a pencil on his desk and waited. In a moment, a bright perky voice materialized on the line.

"Assistant District Attorney Raoul Chabrier," the voice insisted.

"Hello, Rollie, this is Meyer Meyer up here at the 87th," Meyer said. "How's every little thing down there on Chelsea Street?"

"Oh, pretty good, pretty good," Chabrier said, "what have you got for us, a little homicide up there perhaps?"

"No, nothing like that, Rollie," Meyer said.

"A little ax murder perhaps?" Chabrier said.

"No, as a matter of fact, this is something personal," Meyer said.

"Oh-*ho!*" Chabrier said.

"Yeah. Listen, Rollie, what can you do if somebody uses your name?"

"What do you mean?" Chabrier asked.

"In a book."

"Oh-*ho!*" Chabrier said. "Did somebody use your name in a book?"

"Yes."

"In a book about the workings of the police department?"

"No."

"Were you mentioned specifically?"

"No. Well, yes *and* no. What do you mean?"

"Did the book specifically mention Detective 3rd/Grade Meyer . . ."

"Detective *2nd*/Grade," Meyer corrected.

"It specifically mentioned Detective 2nd/Grade Meyer Meyer of the . . ."

"No."

"It *didn't* mention you?"

"No. Not that way."

"I thought you said somebody used your name."

"Well, they did. She did."

"Meyer, I'm a busy man," Chabrier said. "I've got a case load here that would fell a brewer's horse, now would you please tell me what's on your mind?"

"A novel," Meyer said. "It's a novel named *Meyer Meyer.*"

"That is the title of the novel?" Chabrier asked.

"Yes. Can I sue?"

"I'm a criminal lawyer," Chabrier said.

"Yes, but . . ."

"I am not familiar with the law of literary property."

"Yes, but . . ."

"Is it a good book?"

"I don't know," Meyer said. "You see," he said, "I'm a *person*, and this book is about some college professor or something, and he's a short plump fellow . . ."

"I'll have to read it," Chabrier said.

"Will you call me after you've read it?"

"What for?"

"To advise me."

"On what?"

"On whether I can sue or not."

"I'll have to read the law," Chabrier said. "Do I owe you a favor, Meyer?"

"You owe me *six* of them," Meyer said somewhat heatedly, "as for example the several times I could have got you out of bed at three o'clock in the morning when we had real meat here in the squadroom and at great risk to myself I held the suspect until the following morning so you could get your beauty sleep on nights when you had the duty. Now, Rollie, I'm asking a very tiny favor, I don't want to go to the expense of getting some fancy copyright lawyer or whatever the hell, I just want to know whether I can sue somebody who used my name that's on a record in the Department of Health on a birth certificate, can I sue this person who uses my name as the title of a novel, and for a *character* in a novel, when here I am a real *person*, for Christ's sake!"

"Okay, don't get excited," Chabrier said.

"Who's excited?" Meyer said.

"I'll read the law and call you back."

"When?"

"Sometime."

"Maybe if we got somebody in the squadroom sometime when you've got the duty, I'll fly in the face of Miranda-Escobedo again and hold off till morning so you can peacefully snore the night . . ."

"Okay, okay, I'll get back to you tomorrow." Chabrier paused. "Don't you want to know what *time* tomorrow?"

"What time tomorrow?" Meyer asked.

The landlady had arthritis, and she hated winter, and she didn't like cops too well, either. She immediately told Cotton Hawes that there had been other policemen prowling around ever since that big mucky-muck got shot last night, why couldn't they leave a lady alone? Hawes, who had been treated to similar diatribes from every landlady and superintendent along the street, patiently explained that he was only doing his job, and said he knew she would want to co-operate in bringing a murderer to justice. The landlady said the city was rotten and corrupt, and as far as she was concerned they could shoot *all* those damn big mucky-mucks, and she wouldn't lose no sleep over any of them.

Hawes had thus far visited four buildings in a row of identical slum tenements facing the glittering glass and concrete structure that was the city's new Philharmonic Hall. The building, a triumph of design (the acoustics weren't so hot, but what the hell) could be clearly seen from any one of the tenements, the wide marble steps across the avenue offering an unrestricted view of anyone who happened to be standing on them, or coming down them, or going up them. The man who had plunked two rifle slugs into Cowper's head could have done so from *any* of these buildings. The only reason the police department was interested in the exact source of the shots was that the killer might have left some evidence behind him. Evidence is always nice to have in a murder case.

The first thing Hawes asked the landlady was whether she had rented an apartment or a room recently to a tall blond man wearing a hearing aid.

"Yes," the landlady said.

That was a good start. Hawes was an experienced detective, and he recognized immediately that the landlady's affirmative reply was a terribly good start.

"Who?" he asked immediately. "Would you know his name?"

"Yes."

"What's his name?"

"Orecchio. Mort Orecchio."

Hawes took out his pad and began writing. "Orecchio," he said, "Mort. Would you happen to know whether it was Morton or Mortimer or exactly what?"

"Just Mort," the landlady said. "Mort Orecchio. He was Eye-talian."

"How do you know?"

"Anything ending in O is Eye-talian."

"You think so? How about Shapiro?" Hawes suggested.

"What are you, a wise guy?" the landlady said.

"This fellow Orecchio, which apartment did you rent him?"

"A *room*, not an apartment," the landlady said. "Third floor front."

"Facing Philharmonic?"

"Yeah."

"Could I see the room?"

"Sure why not? I got nothing else to do but show cops rooms."

They began climbing. The hallway was cold and the air shaft windows were rimed with frost. There was the commingled smell of garbage and urine on the stairs, a nice clean old lady this landlady. She kept complaining about her arthritis all the way up to the third floor, telling Hawes the cortisone didn't help her none, all them big mucky-muck doctors making promises that didn't help her pain at all. She stopped outside a door with the brass numerals 31 on it, and fished into the pocket of her apron for a key. Down the hall, a door opened a crack and then closed again.

"Who's that?" Hawes asked.

"Who's who?" the landlady said.

"Down the hall there. The door that just opened and closed."

"Musta been Polly," the landlady said, and unlocked the door to 31.

The room was small and cheerless. A three-quarter bed was against the wall opposite the door, covered with a white chenille bedspread. A framed print was over the bed. It showed a logging mill and a river and a sheepdog looking up at something in the sky. A standing floor lamp was on the right of the bed. The shade was yellow and soiled. A stain, either whiskey or vomit, was on the corner of the bedspread where it was pulled up over the pillows. Opposite the bed, there was a single dresser with a mirror over it. The dresser had cigarette burns all the way around its top. The mirror was spotted and peeling. The sink alongside the dresser had a big rust ring near the drain.

"How long was he living here?" Hawes asked.

"Took the room three days ago."

"Did he pay by check or cash?"

"Cash. In advance. Paid for a full week. I only rent by the week, I don't like none of these one-night stands."

"Naturally not," Hawes said.

"I know what you're thinking. You're thinking it ain't such a fancy place, I shouldn't be so fussy. Well, it may not be fancy," the landlady said, "but it's clean."

"Yes, I can see that."

"I mean it ain't go no *bugs*, mister."

Hawes nodded and went to the window. The shade was torn and missing its pull cord. He grabbed the lower edge in his gloved hand, raised the shade and looked across the street.

"You hear any shots last night?"

"No."

He looked down at the floor. There were no spent cartridge cases anywhere in sight.

"Who else lives on this floor?"

"Polly down the hall, that's all."

"Polly who?"

"Malloy."

"Mind if I look through the dresser and the closet?"

"Go right ahead. I got all the time in the world. The way I spend my day is I conduct guided tours through the building."

Hawes went to the dresser and opened each of the drawers. They were all empty, except for a cockroach nestling in the corner of the bottom drawer.

"You missed one," Hawes said, and closed the drawer.

"Huh?" the landlady said.

Hawes went to the closet and opened it. There were seven wire hangers on the clothes bar. The closet was empty. He was about to close the door when something on the floor caught his eye. He stooped for a closer look, took a pen light from his pocket, and turned it on. The object on the floor was a dime.

"If that's money," the landlady said, "it belongs to me."

"Here," Hawes said, and handed her the dime. He did so knowing full well that even if the coin *had* belonged to the occupant of the room, it was as impossible to get latent prints from money as it was to get reimbursed by the city for gasoline used in one's private car on police business.

"Is there a john in here?" he asked.

"Down the hall. Lock the door behind you."

"I only wanted to know if there was another room, that's all."

"It's clean, if that's what you're worrying about."

"I'm sure it's spotless," Hawes said. He took another look around. "So this is it, huh?"

"This is it."

"I'll be sending a man over to dust that sill," Hawes said.

"Why?" the landlady said. "It's clean."

"I mean for fingerprints."

"Oh." The landlady stared at him. "You think that big mucky-muck was shot from this room?"

"It's possible," Hawes said.

"Will that mean trouble for me?"

"Not unless you shot him," Hawes said, and smiled.

"You got some sense of humor," the landlady said.

They went out of the apartment. The landlady locked the door behind her. "Will that be all," she asked, "or did you want to see anything else?"

"I want to talk to the woman down the hall," Hawes said, "but I won't need you for that. Thank you very much, you were very helpful."

"It breaks the monotony," the landlady said, and he believed her.

"Thank you again," he said, and watched her as she went down the steps. He walked to the door marked 32 and knocked. There was no answer. He knocked again and said, "Miss Malloy?"

The door opened a crack.

"Who is it?" a voice said.

"Police officer. May I talk to you?"

"What about?"

"About Mr. Orecchio."

"I don't know any Mr. Orecchio," the voice said.

"Miss Malloy . . ."

"It's *Mrs*. Malloy, and I don't know any Mr. Orecchio."

"Could you open the door, ma'am?"

"I don't want any trouble."

"I won't . . ."

"I know a man got shot last night, I don't want any trouble."

"Did you hear the shots, Miss Malloy?"

"*Mrs.* Malloy."

"Did you?"

"No."

"Would you happen to know if Mr. Orecchio was in last night?"

"I don't know who Mr. Orecchio is."

"The man in 31."

"I don't know him."

"Ma'am, could you please open the door?"

"I don't want to."

"Ma'am, I can come back with a warrant, but it'd be a lot easier . . ."

"Don't get me in trouble," she said. "I'll open the door, but please don't get me in trouble."

Polly Malloy was wearing a pale green cotton wrapper. The wrapper had short sleeves. Hawes saw the hit marks on her arms the moment she opened the door, and the hit marks explained a great deal about the woman who was Polly Malloy. She was perhaps twenty-six years old, with a slender youthful body and a face that would have been pretty if it were not so clearly stamped with knowledge. The green eyes were intelligent and alert, the mouth vulnerable. She worried her lip and held the wrapper closed about her naked body, and her fingers were long and slender, and the hit marks on her arms shouted all there was to shout.

"I'm not holding," she said.

"I didn't ask."

"You can look around if you like."

"I'm not interested," Hawes said.

"Come in," she said.

He went into the apartment. She closed and locked the door behind him.

"I don't want trouble," she said. "I've had enough trouble."

"I won't give you any. I only want to know about the man down the hall."

"I know somebody got shot. Please don't get me involved in it."

They sat opposite each other, she on the bed, he on a straight-backed chair facing her. Something shimmered on the air between them, something as palpable as the tenement stink of garbage and piss surrounding them. They sat in easy informality, comfortably aware of each other's trade, Cotton Hawes detective, Polly Malloy addict. And perhaps they knew each other better than a great many people ever get to know each other. Perhaps Hawes had been inside too many shooting galleries not to understand what it was like to be this girl, perhaps he had arrested too many hookers who were screwing for the couple of bucks they needed for a bag of shit, perhaps he had watched the agonized writhings of too many cold turkey kickers, perhaps his knowledge of this junkie or any junkie was as intimate as a pusher's, perhaps he had seen too much and knew too much. And perhaps the girl had been collared too many times, had protested too many times that she was clean, had thrown too many decks of heroin under bar stools or down sewers at the approach of a cop, had been in too many different squadrooms and handled by too many different bulls, been offered the Lexington choice by too many different magistrates, perhaps her knowledge of the law as it applied to narcotics addicts was as intimate as any assistant district attorney's, perhaps she too had seen too much and knew too much. Their mutual knowledge was electric, it generated a heat lightning of its own, ascertaining the curious symbiosis of lawbreaker and enforcer, affirming the interlocking subtlety of crime and punishment. There was a secret bond in that room, an affinity—almost an empathy. They could talk to each other without any bullshit. They were like spent lovers whispering on the same pillow.

"Did you know Orecchio?" Hawes asked.

"Will you keep me clean?"

"Unless you had something to do with it."

"Nothing."

"You've got my word."

"A cop?" she asked, and smiled wanly.

"You've got my word, if you want it."

"I need it, it looks like."

"You need it, honey."

"I knew him."

"How?"

"I met him the night he moved in."

"When was that?"

"Two, three nights ago."

"Where'd you meet?"

"I was hung up real bad, I needed a fix. I just got out

of Caramoor, *that* sweet hole, a week ago. I haven't had time to get really connected yet."

"What were you in for?"

"Oh, hooking."

"How old are you, Polly?"

"Nineteen. I look older, huh?"

"Yes, you look older."

"I got married when I was sixteen. To another junkie like myself. Some prize."

"What's he doing now?"

"Time at Castleview."

"For what?"

Polly shrugged. "He started pushing."

"Okay, what about Orecchio next door?"

"I asked him for a loan."

"When was this?"

"Day before yesterday."

"Did he give it to you?"

"I didn't actually ask him for a loan. I offered to turn a trick for him. He was right next door, you see, and I was pretty sick, I swear to God I don't think I coulda made it to the street."

"Did he accept?"

"He gave me ten bucks. He didn't take nothing from me for it."

"Sounds like a nice fellow."

Polly shrugged.

"Not a nice fellow?" Hawes asked.

"Let's say not my type," Polly said.

"Mm-huh."

"Let's say a son of a bitch," Polly said.

"What happened?"

"He came in here last night."

"When? What time?"

"Musta been about nine, nine-thirty."

"After the symphony started," Hawes said.

"Huh?"

"Nothing, I was just thinking out loud. Go on."

"He said he had something nice for me. He said if I came into his room, he would give me something nice."

"Did you go?"

"First I asked him what it was. He said it was something I wanted more than anything else in the world."

"But did you go into his room?"

"Yes."

"Did you see anything out of the ordinary?"

"Like what?"

"Like a high-powered rifle with a telescopic sight."

"No, nothing like that."

"All right, what was this 'something nice' he promised you?"

"Hoss."

"He had heroin for you?"

"And that's why he asked you to come into his room? For the heroin?"

"Yes."

"That's what he said."

"He didn't attempt to sell it to you, did he?"

"No. But . . ."

"Yes?"

"He made me beg for it."

"What do you mean?"

"He showed it to me, and he let me taste it to prove that it was real stuff, and then he refused to give it to me unless I . . . begged for it."

"I see."

"He . . . teased me for . . . I guess for . . . for almost two hours. He kept looking at his watch and making me . . . do things."

"What kind of things?"

"Stupid things. He asked me to sing for him. He made me sing 'White Christmas,' that was supposed to be a big joke, you see, because the shit is white and he knew how bad I needed a fix, so he made me sing 'White Christmas' over and over again, I musta sung it for him six or seven times. And all the while he kept looking at his watch."

"Go ahead."

"Then he . . . he asked me to strip, but . . . I mean, not just take off my clothes, but . . . you know, do a strip for him. And I did it. And he began . . . he began making fun of me, of the way I looked, of my body. I . . . he made me stand naked in front of him, and he just went on and on about how stupid and pathetic I looked, and he kept asking me if I really wanted the heroin, and then looked at his watch again, it was about eleven o'clock by then, I kept saying Yes, I want it, please let me have it, so he asked me to dance for him, he asked me to do the waltz, and then he asked me to do the shag, I didn't know what the hell he was talking about, I never even heard of the shag, have you ever heard of the shag?"

"Yes, I've heard of it," Hawes said.

"So I did all that for him, I would have done anything for him, and finally he told me to get on my knees and explain to him why I felt I really needed the bag of heroin. He said he expected me to talk for five minutes on the subject of the addict's need for narcotics, and he looked at his watch and began timing me, and I talked. I was shaking by this time, I had the chills, I needed a shot more than . . ." Polly closed her eyes. "I began crying. I talked and I cried, and at last he looked at his watch and said, 'Your five minutes are up. Here's your poison, now get the hell out of here.' And he threw the bag to me."

"What time was this?"

"It musta been about ten minutes after eleven. I don't have a watch, I hocked it long ago, but you can see the big electric numbers on top of the Mutual Building from my room, and when I was shooting up later it was 11:15, so this musta been about ten after or thereabouts."

"And he kept looking at his watch all through this, huh?"

"Yes. As if he had a date or something."

"He did," Hawes said.

"Huh?"

"He had a date to shoot a man from his window. He was just amusing himself until the concert broke. A nice fellow, Mr. Oreccho."

"I got to say one thing for him," Polly said.

"What's that?"

"It was good stuff." A wistful look came onto her face and into her eyes. "It was some of the best stuff I've had in years. I wouldn't have heard a *cannon* if it went off next door."

Hawes made a routine check of all the city's telephone directories, found no listing for an Orecchio—Mort, Morton, or Mortimer—and then called the Bureau of Criminal Identification at four o'clock that afternoon. The B.C.I., fully automated, called back within ten minutes to report that they had nothing on the suspect. Hawes then sent a teletype to the F.B.I. in Washington, asking them to check their voluminous files for any known criminal named Orecchio, Mort or Mortimer or Morton. He was sitting at his desk in the paint-smelling squadroom when Patrolman Richard Genero came up to ask whether he had to go to court with Kling on the collar they had made jointly and together the week before. Genero had been walking his beat all afternoon, and he was very cold, so he hung around long after Hawes had answered his question, hoping he would be offered a cup of coffee. His eye happened to fall on the name Hawes had scribbled onto his desk pad when calling the B.C.I., so Genero decided to make a quip.

"Another Italian suspect, I see," he said.

"How do you know?" Hawes asked.

"Anything ending in O is Italian," Genero said.

"How about Munro?" Hawes asked.

"What are you, a wise guy?" Genero said, and grinned. He looked at the scribbled name again, and then said, "I got to admit *this* guy has a very funny name for an Italian."

"Funny how?" Hawes asked.

"Ear," Genero said.

"What?"

"Ear. That's what Orecchio means in Italian. Ear."

Which when coupled with Mort, of course, could mean nothing more or less than Dead Ear.

Hawes tore the page from the pad, crumpled it into a ball, and threw it at the wastebasket, missing.

"I said something?" Genero asked, knowing he'd never get his cup of coffee now.

5

THE BOY WHO DELIVERED THE NOTE WAS EIGHT YEARS old, and he had instructions to give it to the desk sergeant. He stood in the squadroom now surrounded by cops who looked seven feet tall, all of them standing around him in a circle while he looked up with saucer-wide blue eyes and wished he was dead.

"Who gave you this note?" one of the cops asked.

"A man in the park."

"Did he pay you to bring it here?"

"Yeah. Yes. Yeah."

"How much?"

"Five dollars."

"What did he look like?"

"He had yellow hair."

"Was he tall?"

"Oh, yeah."

"Was he wearing a hearing aid?"

"Yeah. A *what*?"

"A thing in his ear."

"Oh, yeah," the kid said.

Everybody tiptoed around the note very carefully, as though it might explode at any moment. Everybody handled the note with tweezers or white cotton gloves. Everybody agreed it should be sent at once to the police lab. Everybody read it at least twice. Everybody studied it and examined it. Even some patrolmen from downstairs came up to have a look at it. It was a very important document. It demanded at least an hour of valuable police time before it was finally encased in a celluloid folder and sent downtown in a manila envelope.

Everybody decided that what this note meant was that the deaf man (who they now reluctantly admitted was once again in their midst) wanted fifty thousand dollars in lieu of killing the deputy mayor exactly as he had killed the parks commissioner. Since fifty thousand dollars was

considerably more than the previous demand for five
thousand dollars, the cops of the 87th were quite right-
fully incensed by the demand. Moreover, the audacity
of this criminal somewhere out there was something
beyond the ken of their experience. For all its resem-
blance to a kidnaping, with its subsequent demand for
ransom, this case was *not* a kidnaping. No one had been
abducted, there was nothing to ransom. No, this was
very definitely extortion, and yet the extortion cases
they'd dealt with over the years had been textbook
cases involving "a wrongful use of force or fear" in an
attempt to obtain "property from another." The key
word was "another." "Another" was invariably the
person against whom mayhem had been threatened. In
this case, though, their extortionist didn't seem to care
who paid the money so long as someone did. *Anyone.*
Now how were you supposed to deal with a maniac like
that?

"He's a maniac," Lieutenant Byrnes said. "Where the
hell does he expect us to get fifty thousand dollars?"

Steve Carella, who had been released from the hospital that afternoon and who somewhat resembled a
boxer about to put on gloves, what with assorted band-
ages taped around his hands, said, "Maybe he expects
the deputy mayor to pay it."

"Then why the hell didn't he *ask* the deputy mayor?"

"We're his intermediaries," Carella said. "He as-
sumes his demand will carry more weight if it comes
from law enforcement officers."

Byrnes looked at Carella.

"Sure," Carella said. "Also, he's getting even with us.

He's sore because we fouled up his bank-robbing scheme eight years ago. This is his way of getting back."

"He's a maniac," Byrnes insisted.

"No, he's a very smart cookie," Carella said. "He knocked off Cowper after a measly demand for five thousand dollars. Now that we know he can do it, he's asking ten times the price not to shoot the deputy mayor."

"Where does it say 'shoot'?" Hawes asked.

"Hmmm?"

"He didn't say anything about *shooting* Scanlon. The note yesterday just said 'Deputy Mayor Scanlon Goes Next.' "

"That's right," Carella said. "He can poison him or bludgeon him or stab him or . . ."

"Please," Byrnes said.

"Let's call Scanlon," Carella suggested. "Maybe he's got fifty grand laying around he doesn't know what to do with."

They called Deputy Mayor Scanlon and advised him of the threat upon his life, but Deputy Mayor Scanlon did not have fifty grand laying around he didn't know what to do with. Ten minutes later, the phone on Byrnes' desk rang. It was the police commissioner.

"All right, Byrnes," the commissioner said sweetly, "what's this latest horseshit?"

"Sir," Byrnes said, "we have had two notes from the man we suspect killed Parks Commissioner Cowper, and they constitute a threat upon the life of Deputy Mayor Scanlon."

"What are you doing about it?" the commissioner asked.

"Sir," Byrnes said, "we have already sent both notes to the police laboratory for analysis. Also, sir, we have located the room from which the shots were fired last night, and we have reason to believe we are dealing with a criminal known to this precinct."

"Who?"

"We don't know."

"I thought you said he was known . . ."

"Yes, sir, we've dealt with him before, but to our knowledge, sir, he is unknown."

"How much money does he want this time?"

"Fifty thousand dollars, sir."

"When is Scanlon supposed to be killed?"

"We don't know, sir."

"When does this man want his money?"

"We don't know, sir."

"Where are you supposed to deliver it?"

"We don't know, sir."

"What the hell *do* you know, Byrnes?"

"I know, sir, that we are doing our best to cope with an unprecedented situation, and that we are ready to put our entire squad at the deputy mayor's disposal, if and when he asks for protection. Moreover, sir, I'm sure I can persuade Captain Frick who, as you may know, commands this entire precinct . . ."

"What do you mean, *as* I may know, Byrnes?"

"That is the way we do it in this city, sir."

"That is the way they do it in *most* cities, Byrnes."

"Yes, sir, of course. In any case, I'm sure I can persuade him to release some uniformed officers from their regular duties, or perhaps to call in some off-duty officers, if the commissioner feels that's necessary."

"I feel it's necessary to protect the life of the deputy mayor."

"Yes, of course, sir, we all feel that," Byrnes said.

"What's the matter, Byrnes, don't you like me?" the commissioner asked.

"I try to keep personal feelings out of my work, sir," Byrnes said. "This is a tough case. I don't know about you, but I've never come up against anything like it before. I've got a good team here, and we're doing our best. More than that, we can't do."

"Byrnes," the commissioner said, "you may *have* to do more."

"Sir . . ." Byrnes started, but the commissioner had hung up.

Arthur Brown sat in the basement of Junior High School 106, with a pair of earphones on his head and his right hand on the start button of a tape recorder. The telephone at the La Bresca house diagonally across the street from the school had just rung for the thirty-second time that day, and as he waited for Concetta La Bresca to lift the receiver (as she had done on thirty-one previous occasions) he activated the recorder and sighed in anticipation of what was to come.

It was very clever of the police to have planted a bug in the La Bresca apartment, that bug having been installed by a plainclothes cop from the lab who identified himself as a telephone repairman, did his dirty work in the La Bresca living room, and then strung his overhead wires from the roof of the La Bresca house to the telephone pole outside, and from there to the pole on the school sidewalk, and from there to the roof of the school building, and down the side wall, and into a basement window, and across the basement floor to a tiny room containing stacked textbooks and the school's old sixteen-millimeter sound projector, where he had set up Arthur Brown's monitoring station.

It was also very clever of the police to have assigned Arthur Brown to this eavesdropping plant because Brown was an experienced cop who had conducted wiretaps before and who was capable of separating the salient from the specious in any given telephone conversation.

There was only one trouble.

Arthur Brown did not understand Italian, and Concetta La Bresca spoke to her friends exclusively in Italian. For all Brown knew, they might have plotted anything from abortion to safe cracking thirty-one times that day, and for all he knew were about to plot it yet another time. He had used up two full reels of tape because he hadn't understood a word that was said, and he wanted each conversation recorded so that someone—probably Carella—could later translate them.

"Hello," a voice said in English.

Brown almost fell off his stool. He sat erect, adjusted the headset, adjusted the volume control on the tape recorder, and began listening.

"Tony?" a second voice asked.

"Yeah, who's this?" The first voice belonged to La Bresca. Apparently he had just returned home from work. The second voice . . .

"This is Dom."

"Who?"

"Dominick."

"Oh, hi, Dom, how's it going?"

"Great."

"What's up, Dom?"

"Oh, nothing," Dom said. "I was just wondering how you was, that's all."

There was silence on the line. Brown tilted his head and brought his hand up to cover one of the earphones.

"I'm fine," La Bresca said at last.

"Good, good," Dom said.

Again, there was silence.

"Well, if that was all you wanted," La Bresca said, "I guess . . ."

"Actually, Tony, I was wondering . . ."

"Yeah?"

"I was wondering if you could lend me a couple of bills till I get myself organized here."

"Organized doing what?" La Bresca asked.

"Well, I took a big loss on the fight two weeks ago, you know, and I still ain't organized."

"You never been organized in your life," La Bresca said.

"That ain't true, Tony."

"Okay, it ain't true. What *is* true is I ain't got a couple of bills to lend you."

"Well, I heard different," Dom said.

"Yeah? What'd you hear?"

"The rumble is you're coming into some very big loot real soon."

"Yeah? Where'd you hear *that* shit?"

"Oh, I listen around here and there, I'm always on the earie."

"Well, this time the rumble is wrong."

"I was thinking maybe just a few C-notes to tide me over for the next week or so. Till I get organized."

"Dom, I ain't seen a C-note since Hector was a pup."

"Tony . . ."

There was a slight hesitation, only long enough to carry the unmistakable weight of warning. Brown caught the suddenly ominous note and listened expectantly for Dom's next words.

"I *know*," Dom said.

There was another silence on the line. Brown waited. He could hear one of the men breathing heavily.

"*What* do you know?" La Bresca asked.

"About the caper."

"*What* caper?"

"Tony, don't let me say it on the phone, huh? You never know who's listening these days."

"What the hell are you trying to do?" La Bresca asked. "Shake me down?"

"No, I'm trying to borrow a couple of hundred is all. Until I get organized. I'd hate like hell to see all your planning go down the drain, Tony. I'd really hate to see that happen."

"You blow the whistle, pal, and we'll know just who done it."

"Tony, if *I* found out about the caper, there's lots of other guys also know about it. It's all over the street. You're lucky the fuzz aren't onto you already."

"The cops don't even know I exist," La Bresca said. "I never took a fall for nothing in my life."

"What you took a fall for and what you done are two different things, right, Tony?"

"Don't bug me, Dom. You screw this up . . ."

"I ain't screwing nothing up. I'm asking for a loan of two hundred bucks, now yes or no, Tony, I'm getting impatient here in this goddamn phone booth. Yes or no?"

"You're a son of a bitch," La Bresca said.

"Does that mean yes?"

"Where do we meet?" La Bresca asked.

Lying in the alleyway that night with his bandaged hands encased in woolen gloves, Carella thought less often of the two punks who had burned him, and also burned him up, than he did about the deaf man.

As he lay in his tattered rags and mildewed shoes, he was the very model of a modern major derelict, hair matted, face streaked, breath stinking of cheap wine. But beneath that torn and threadbare coat, Carella's gloved right hand held a .38 Detective's Special. The right index finger of the glove had been cut away to the knuckle, allowing Carella to squeeze the finger itself inside the trigger guard. He was ready to shoot, and this time he would not allow himself to be cold-cocked. Or even pan-broiled.

But whereas his eyes were squinted in simulated drunken slumber while alertly he watched the alley mouth and listened for tandem footsteps, his thoughts were on the deaf man. He did not like thinking about the deaf man because he could remember with painful clarity the shotgun blast fired at him eight years ago, the excruciating pain in his shoulder, the numbness of his arm and hand, and then the repeated smashing of the shotgun's stock against his face until he fell senseless to the floor. He did not like thinking about how close he had come to death at the hands of the deaf man. Nor did he enjoy thinking of a criminal adversary who was really quite smarter than any of the detectives on the 87th Squad, a schemer, a planner, a brilliant bastard who juggled life and death with the dexterity and emotional sang-froid of a mathematician. The deaf man—somewhere out there—was a machine, and Carella was terrified of things that whirred with computer precision, logical but unreasoning, infallible and aloof, cold and deadly. He dreaded the thought of going up against him once again, and yet he knew this stakeout was small potatoes, two punks itching to get caught, two punks who *would* be caught because they assumed all their intended victims were defenseless and did not realize that one of them could be a detective with his finger curled around the trigger of a deadly weapon. And once they were caught, he would move from the periphery of the deaf man case into the very nucleus of the case itself. And perhaps, once again, come face to face with the tall blond man who wore the hearing aid.

He thought it oddly coincidental and perfectly ironic that the person he loved most in the world was a woman named Teddy Carella, who happened to be his wife, and who also happened to be a deaf mute, whereas the person who frightened him most as a cop and as a man was also deaf, or at least purported to be so, advertised it blatantly—or was this only another subterfuge, a part of the overall scheme? The terrifying thing about the deaf man was his confident assumption that he was dealing with a bunch of nincompoops. Perhaps he was. That was *another* terrifying thing about him. He moved with such certainty that his assumptions took on all the aspects of cold fact. If he said that all flatfoots were fools, then by God that's exactly what they must be—better pay the man whatever he wants before he kills off every high-ranking official in the city. If he could outrageously outline a murder scheme and then execute it before the startled eyes of the city's finest, how could he possibly be stopped from committing the *next* murder, or the one after that, or the one after that?

Carella did not enjoy feeling like a fool.

There were times when he did not necessarily enjoy police work (like right now, freezing his ass off in an alley) but there were never times when he lacked respect for what he did. The concept of law enforcement was simple and clear in his mind. The good guys against the bad guys. He was one of the good guys. And whereas the bad guys in this day and age won often enough to make virtue seem terribly unfashionable sometimes, Carella nonetheless felt that killing people (for example) was not a very nice thing. Nor was breaking into someone's dwelling place in the nighttime overly considerate. Nor was pushing dope quite thoughtful. Nor were mugging, or forging, or kidnaping, or pimping (or spitting on the sidewalk, for that matter) civilized acts designed to uplift the spirit or delight the soul.

He was a cop.

Which meant that he was stuck with all the various images encouraged by countless television shows and motion pictures: the dim-witted public servant being outsmarted by the tough private eye; the overzealous jerk inadvertently blocking the attempts of the intelligent young advertising executive in distress; the insensitive dolt blindly encouraging the young to become adult criminals. Well, what're you gonna do? You got an image, you got one. (He wondered how many television writers were lying in an alley tonight waiting for two hoods to attack.) The damn thing about the deaf man, though, was that he made all these stereotypes seem true. Once he appeared on the scene, every cop on the squad *did* appear dim-witted and bumbling and inefficient.

And if a man could do that merely by making a few phone calls or sending a few notes, what would happen if—

Carella tensed.

The detective assigned to the surveillance of Anthony La Bresca was Bert Kling, whom he had never seen before. Brown's call to the squadroom had advised the lieutenant that La Bresca had admitted he was involved in a forthcoming caper, and this was reason enough to put a tail on him. So Kling took to the sub-zero streets, leaving the warmth and generosity of Cindy's apartment, and drove out to Riverhead, where he waited across the street from La Bresca's house, hoping to pick up his man the moment he left to meet Dominick. Brown had informed the lieutenant that the pair had arranged a meeting for ten o'clock that night, and it was now 9:07 by Kling's luminous dial, so he figured he had got here good and early, just in time to freeze solid.

La Bresca came down the driveway on the right of the stucco house at ten minutes to ten. Kling stepped into the shadows behind his parked car. La Bresca began walking east, toward the elevated train structure two blocks away. Just my luck, Kling thought, he hasn't got a car. He gave him a lead of half a block, and then began following him. A sharp wind was blowing west off the wide avenue ahead. Kling was forced to lift his face to its direct blast every so often because he didn't want to lose sight of La Bresca, and he cursed for perhaps the fifty-seventh time that winter the injustice of weather designed to plague a man who worked outdoors. Not that he worked outdoors all of the time. Part of the time, he worked at a desk typing up reports in triplicate or calling victims or witnesses. But *much* of the time (it was fair to say much of the time) he worked outdoors, legging it here and there all over this fair city, asking questions and compiling answers and this was the worst son of a bitch winter he had ever lived through in his life. I hope you're going someplace nice and warm, La Bresca, he thought. I hope you're going to meet your friend at a Turkish bath or someplace.

Ahead, La Bresca was climbing the steps to the elevated platform. He glanced back at Kling only once,
and Kling immediately ducked his head, and then
quickened his pace. He did not want to reach the platform to discover that La Bresca had already boarded a
train and disappeared.

He need not have worried. La Bresca was waiting
for him near the change booth.

"You following me?" he asked.

"What?" Kling said.

"I *said* are you following me?" La Bresca asked.

The choices open to Kling in that moment were severely limited. He could say, "What are you out of
your mind, why would I be following you, you're so
handsome or something?" Or he could say, "Yes, I'm
following you, I'm a police officer, here's my shield
and my I.D. card," those were the open choices. Either
way, the tail was blown.

"You looking for a rap in the mouth?" Kling said.

"What?" La Bresca said, startled.

"I said what are you, some kind of paranoid nut?"
Kling said, which wasn't what he had said at all. La
Bresca didn't seem to notice the discrepancy. He
stared at Kling in honest surprise, and then started to
mumble something, which Kling cut short with a
glowering, menacing, thoroughly frightening look.
Mumbling himself, Kling went up the steps to the uptown side of the platform. The station stop was dark
and deserted and windswept. He stood on the platform
with his coattails flapping about him, and waited until
La Bresca came up the steps on the downtown side. La

Bresca's train pulled in not three minutes later, and he boarded it. The train rattled out of the station. Kling went downstairs again and found a telephone booth. When Willis picked up the phone at the squadroom, Kling said, "This is Bert. La Bresca made me a couple of blocks from his house. You'd better get somebody else on him."

"How long you been a cop?" Willis asked.

"It happens to the best of us," Kling said. "Where'd Brown say they were meeting?"

"A bar on Crawford."

"Well, he boarded a downtown train just a few minutes ago, you've got time to plant somebody there before he arrives."

"Yeah, I'll get O'Brien over there right away."

"What do you want me to do, come back to the office or what?"

"How the hell did you manage to get spotted?"

"Just lucky, I guess," Kling said.

It was one of those nights.

They came into the alley swiftly, moving directly toward Carella, both of them boys of about seventeen or eighteen, both of them brawny, one of them carrying a large tin can, the label gone from it, the can catching light from the street lamp, glinting in the alleyway as they approached, that's the can of gasoline, Carella thought.

He started to draw his gun and for the first time ever in the history of his career as a cop, it snagged.

It snagged somewhere inside his coat. It was supposed to be a gun designed for negligible bulk, it was not supposed to catch on your goddamn clothing, the two-inch barrel was not supposed to snag when you pulled it, here we go, he thought, the Keystone cops, and leaped to his feet. He could not get the damn gun loose, it was tangled in the wool of his slipover sweater, the yarn pulling and unraveling, he knew the can of gasoline would be thrown into his face in the next moment, he knew a match or a lighter would flare into life, this time they'd be able to smell burning flesh away the hell back at the squadroom. Instinctively, he brought his left hand down as straight and as rigid as a steel pipe, slammed it down onto the forearm of the boy with the can, hitting it hard enough to shatter bone, hearing the scream that erupted from the boy's mouth as he dropped the can, and then feeling the intense pain that rocketed into his head and almost burst from his own lips as his burned and bandaged hand reacted. This is great, he thought, I have no hands, they're going to beat the shit out of me, which turned out to be a fairly good prediction because that's exactly what they did.

There was no danger from the gasoline now, small consolation, at least they couldn't set fire to him. But his hands were useless, and his gun was snagged somewhere inside there on his sweater—he tried ripping the tangled yarn free, ten seconds, twenty seconds, a millennium—and his attackers realized instantly that they had themselves a pigeon, so they all jumped on him, all forty guys in the alley, and then it was too late. They were very good street fighters, these boys. They had learned all about punching to the Adam's apple, they had learned all about flanking operations, one circling around to his left and the other coming up behind to clout him on the back of the head with the neatest rabbit's punch he had ever taken, oh, they were nice fighters, these boys, he wondered whether the coffin would be metal or wood. While he was wondering this, one of the boys who had learned how to fight in some clean friendly slum, kicked him in the groin, which can hurt. Carella doubled over, and the other clean fighter behind him delivered a second rabbit punch, rabbit punches doubtless being his specialty, while the lad up front connected with a good hard-swinging uppercut that almost tore off his head. So now he was down on the alley floor, the alley covered with refuse and grime and not a little of his own blood, so they decided to stomp him, which is of course what you must necessarily do when your opponent falls down, you kick him in the head and the shoulders and the chest and everywhere you can manage to kick him. If he's a live one, he'll squirm around and try to grab your feet, but if you happen to be lucky enough to get a pigeon who was burned only recently, why you can have an absolute field day kicking him at will because his hands are too tender to grab at *anything*, no less feet. That's why guns were invented, Carella thought, so that if you happen to have second-degree burns on your hands you don't have to use them too much, all you have to do is squeeze a trigger, it's a shame the gun snagged. It's a shame, too, that Teddy's going to be collecting a widow's dole tomorrow morning, he thought, but these guys are going to kill me unless I do something pretty fast. The trouble is I'm a bumbling god-damn cop, the deaf man is right. The kicks landed now with increasing strength and accuracy, nothing encourages a stomper more than an inert and increasingly more vulnerable victim. I'm certainly glad the gasoline, he thought, and a kick exploded against his left eye. He thought at once he would lose the eye, he saw only a blinding flash of yellow, he rolled away, feeling dizzy and nauseous, a boot collided with his rib, he thought he felt it crack, another kick landed on the kneecap of his left leg, he tried to get up, his hands, "You fucking fuzz," one of the boys said, Fuzz, he thought, and was suddenly sick, and another kick crashed into the back of his skull and sent him falling face forward into his own vomit.

He lost consciousness.

He might have been dead, for all he knew.

It was one of those nights.

Bob O'Brien got a flat tire on the way to the Erin Bar & Grill on Crawford Avenue, where Tony La Bresca was to meet the man named Dom.

By the time he changed the flat, his hands were numb, his temper was short, the time was 10:32, and the bar was still a ten-minute drive away. On the off-chance that La Bresca and his fair-weather friend would still be there, O'Brien drove downtown, arriving at the bar at ten minutes to eleven. Not only were they both gone already, but the bartender said to O'Brien the moment he bellied up, "Care for something to drink, Officer?"

It was one of those nights.

ON FRIDAY MORNING, MARCH 8, DETECTIVE-LIEUTENANT
Sam Grossman of the Police Laboratory called the
squadroom and asked to talk to Cotton Hawes. He was
informed that Hawes, together with several other detectives on the squad, had gone to Buena Vista Hospital to
visit Steve Carella. The man answering the telephone
was Patrolman Genero, who was holding the fort until
one of them returned.

"Well, do *you* want this information or what?"
Grossman asked.

"Sir, I'm just supposed to record any calls till they get
back," Genero said.

"I'm going to be tied up later," Grossman said, "why
don't I just give this to you?"

"All right, sir," Genero said, and picked up his
pencil. He felt very much like a detective. Besides, he

was grateful not to be outside on another miserable day like this one. "Shoot," he said, and quickly added, "Sir."

"It's on those notes I received."

"Yes, sir, what notes?"

"'Deputy Mayor Scanlon goes next,'" Grossman quoted, "and 'Look! A whole new,' et cetera."

"Yes, sir," Genero said, not knowing what Grossman was talking about.

"The paper is Whiteside Bond, available at any stationery store in the city. The messages were clipped from national magazines and metropolitan dailies. The adhesive is rubber cement."

"Yes, sir," Genero said, writing frantically.

"Negative on latent prints. We got a whole mess of smeared stuff, but nothing we could run a make on."

"Yes, sir."

"In short," Grossman said, "you know what you can do with these notes."

"What's that, sir?" Genero asked.

"We only run the tests," Grossman said. "*You* guys are supposed to come up with the answers."

Genero beamed. He had been included in the phrase "You guys" and felt himself to be a part of the elite. "Well, thanks a lot," he said, "we'll get to work on it up here."

"Right," Grossman said. "You want these notes back?"

"No harm having them."

"I'll send them over," Grossman said, and hung up.

Very interesting, Genero thought, replacing the receiver on its cradle. If he had owned a deerstalker hat, he would have put it on in that moment.

"Where's the john?" one of the painters asked.

"Why?" Genero said.

"We have to paint it."

"Try not to slop up the urinals," Genero said.

"We're Harvard men," the painter said. "We never slop up the urinals."

The other painter laughed.

The third note arrived at eleven o'clock that morning. It was delivered by a high school dropout who walked directly past the muster desk and up to the squadroom where Patrolman Genero was evolving an elaborate mystery surrounding the rubber cement that had been used as an adhesive.

"What's everybody on vacation?" the kid asked. He was seventeen years old, his face sprinkled with acne. He felt very much at home in a squadroom because he had once been a member of a street gang called The Terrible Ten, composed of eleven young men who had joined together to combat Puerto Rican influx into their turf. The gang had disbanded just before Christmas, not because the Puerto Ricans had managed to demolish them, but only because seven of the eleven called The Terrible Ten had finally succumbed to an enemy common to Puerto Rican and white Anglo-Saxon alike: narcotics. Five of the seven were hooked, two were dead. Of the remaining three, one was in prison for gun violation, another had got married because he'd knocked up a little Irish girl, and the last was carrying an envelope into a detective squadroom, and feeling comfortable enough there to make a quip to a uniformed cop.

"What do you want?" Genero asked.

"I was supposed to give this to the desk sergeant, but there's nobody at the desk. You want to take it?"

"What is it?"

"Search me," the kid said. "Guy stopped me on the street and give me five bucks to deliver it."

"Sit down," Genero said. He took the envelope from the kid and debated opening it, and then realized he had got his fingerprints all over it. He dropped it on the desk. In the toilet down the hall, the painters were singing. Genero was only supposed to answer the phone and take down messages. He looked at the envelope again, severely tempted. "I said sit down," he told the kid.

"What for?"

"You're going to wait here until one of the detectives gets back, that's what for."

"Up yours, fuzz," the kid said, and turned to go.

Genero drew his service revolver. "Hey," he said, and the boy glanced over his shoulder into the somewhat large bore of a .38 Police Special.

"I'm hip to Miranda-Escobedo," the kid said, but he sat down nonetheless.

"Good, that makes two of us," Genero said.

Cops don't like other cops to get it. It makes them nervous. It makes them feel they are in a profession that is not precisely white collar, despite the paperwork involved. It makes them feel that at any moment someone might hit them or kick them or even shoot them.

It makes them feel unloved.

The two young sportsmen who had unloved Carella so magnificently had broken three of his ribs and his nose. They had also given him such a headache, due to concussion caused by a few well-placed kicks to the medulla oblongata. He had gained consciousness shortly after being admitted to the hospital and he was conscious now, of course, but he didn't look good, and he didn't feel good, and he didn't feel much like talking. So he sat with Teddy beside the bed, holding her hand and breathing shallowly because the broken ribs hurt like hell. The detectives did most of the talking, but there was a cheerlessness in their banter. They were suddenly face to face with violence of a most personal sort, not the violence they dealt with every working day of their lives, not an emotionless confrontation with broken mutilated strangers, but instead a glimpse at a friend and colleague who lay in battered pain on a hospital bed while his wife held his hand and tried to smile at their feeble jokes.

The four detectives left the hospital room at twelve noon. Brown and Willis walked ahead of Hawes and Kling, who trailed behind them silently.

"Man, they got him good," Brown said.

The seventeen-year-old dropout was beginning to scream Miranda-Escobedo, quoting rights like a lawyer. Genero kept telling him to shut up, but he had never really understood the Supreme Court decision too well, despite the flyers issued to every cop in the precinct, and he was afraid now that the kid knew something he didn't know. He was overjoyed to hear the ring of footsteps on the recently painted iron-runged steps leading to the squadroom. Willis and Brown came into view on the landing first. Kling and Hawes were behind them. Genero could have kissed them all.

"These the bulls?" the dropout asked, and Genero said, "Shut up."

"What's up?" Brown asked.

"Tell your friend here about Miranda-Escobedo," the kid said.

"Who're you?" Brown asked.

"He delivered an envelope," Genero said.

"Here we go," Hawes said.

"What's your name, kid?"

"Give me some advice on my rights," the kid said.

"Tell me your name, or I'll kick your ass in," Brown said. "How do you like *that* advice?" He had just witnessed what a pair of young hoods had done to Carella, and he was in no mood to take nonsense from a snot-nose.

"My name is Michael McFadden, and I won't answer no questions without a lawyer here," the kid said.

"Can you afford a lawyer?" Brown asked.

"No."

"Get him a lawyer, Hal," Brown said, bluffing.

"Hey, wait a minute, what is this?" McFadden asked.

"You want a lawyer, we'll get you a lawyer," Brown said.

"What do I need a lawyer for? All I done was deliver an envelope."

"*I* don't know why you need a lawyer," Brown said.

"*You're* the one who said you wanted one. Hal, call the D.A.'s office, get this suspect here a lawyer."

"Suspect?" McFadden said, "*Suspect?* What the hell did *I* do?"

"I don't know, kid," Brown said, "and I can't find out because you won't let me ask any questions without a lawyer here. You getting him that lawyer, Hal?"

Willis, who had lifted the phone receiver and was listening to nothing more vital than a dial tone, said, "Tie-line's busy, Art."

"Okay, I guess we'll just have to wait then. Make yourself comfortable, kid, we'll get a lawyer up here for you soon as we can."

"Look, what the hell," McFadden said, "I don't need no lawyer."

"You said you wanted one."

"Yeah, but, I mean, like if this is nothing serious . . ."

"We just wanted to ask you some questions about that envelope, that's all."

"Why? What's in it?"

"Let's open the envelope and show the kid what's in it, shall we do that?" Brown said.

"All I done was deliver it," McFadden said.

"Well, let's see what's inside it, shall we?" Brown said. He folded his handkerchief over the envelope, slit it open with a letter opener, and then used a tweezer to yank out the folded note.

"Here, use these," Kling said, and took a pair of white cotton gloves from the top drawer of his desk. Brown put on the gloves, held his hands widespread alongside his face, and grinned.

"Whuffo does a chicken cross de road, Mistuh Bones?" he said, and burst out laughing. The other cops all laughed with him. Encouraged, McFadden laughed too. Brown glowered at him, and the laugh died in his throat. Gingerly, Brown unfolded the note and spread it flat on the desk top:

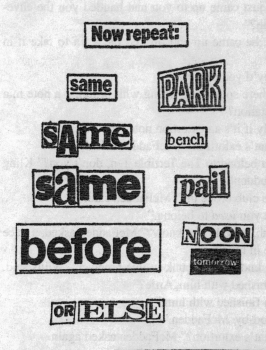

"What's that supposed to mean?" McFadden asked.

"You tell us," Brown said.

"Beats me."

"Who gave you this note?"

"A tall blond guy wearing a hearing aid."

"You know him?"

"Never saw him before in my life."

"He just came up to you and handed you the envelope, huh?"

"No, he came up and offered me a fin to take it in here."

"Why'd you accept?"

"Is there something wrong with bringing a note in a police station?"

"Only if it's an extortion note," Brown said.

"What's extortion?" McFadden asked.

"You belong to The Terrible Ten, don't you?" Kling asked suddenly.

"The club broke up," McFadden said.

"But you *used* to belong."

"Yeah, how do you know?" McFadden asked, a trace of pride in his voice.

"We know every punk in this precinct," Willis said. "You finished with him, Artie?"

"I'm finished with him."

"Good-by, McFadden."

"What's extortion?" McFadden asked again.

"Good-by," Willis said again.

The detective assigned to tailing Anthony La Bresca was Meyer Meyer. He was picked for the job because detectives aren't supposed to be bald, and it was reasoned that La Bresca, already gun shy, would never tip to him. It was further reasoned that if La Bresca was really involved in a contemplated caper, it might be best not to follow him from his job to wherever he was going, but instead to be waiting for him there when he arrived. This presented the problem of second-guessing where he might be going, but it was recalled by one or another of the detectives that La Bresca had mentioned frequenting a pool hall on South Leary, and so this was where Meyer stationed himself at four o'clock that afternoon.

He was wearing baggy corduroy trousers, a brown leather jacket, and a brown watch cap. He looked like a longshoreman or something. Actually, he didn't know what he looked like, he just hoped he didn't look like a cop. He had a matchstick in his mouth. He figured that was a nice touch, the matchstick. Also, because criminal types have an uncanny way of knowing when somebody is heeled, he was not carrying a gun. The only weapon on his person was a longshoreman's hook tucked into the waistband of his trousers. If anyone asked him about the hook, he would say he needed it on the job, thereby establishing his line of work at the same time. He hoped he would not have to use the hook.

He wandered into the pool hall, which was on the second floor of a dingy brick building, said "Hi," to the man sitting behind the entrance booth, and then said, "You got any open tables?"

"Pool or billiards?" the man said. He was chewing on a matchstick, too.

"Pool," Meyer said.

"Take Number Four," the man said, and turned to switch on the table lights from the panel behind him. "You new around here?" he asked, his back to Meyer.

"Yeah, I'm new around here," Meyer said.

"We don't dig hustlers," the man said.

"I'm no hustler," Meyer answered.

"Just make sure you ain't."

Meyer shrugged and walked over to the lighted table. There were seven other men in the pool hall, all of them congregated around a table near the windows, where four of them were playing and the other three were kibitzing. Meyer unobtrusively took a cue from the rack, set up the balls, and began shooting. He was a lousy player. He kept mentally calling shots and missing. Every now and then he glanced at the door. He was playing for perhaps ten minutes when one of the men from the other table sauntered over.

"Hi," the man said. He was a burly man wearing a sports jacket over a woolen sports shirt. Tufts of black hair showed above the open throat of the shirt. His eyes were a deep brown, and he wore a black mustache that seemed to have leaped from his chest onto the space below his nose. The hair on his head was black too. He looked tough and he looked menacing, and Meyer immediately made him for the local cheese.

"You play here before?" the man asked.

"Nope," Meyer said without looking up from the table.

"I'm Tino."

"Hello, Tino," Meyer said, and shot.

"You missed," Tino said.

"That's right, I did."

"You a hustler?" Tino said.

"Nope."

"We break hustlers' arms and throw them down the stairs," Tino said.

"The arms or the whole hustler?" Meyer asked.

"I got no sense of humor," Tino said.

"Me, neither. Buzz off, you're ruining my game."

"Don't try to take nobody, mister," Tino said. "This's a friendly neighborhood pool hall."

"Yeah, you sure make it sound very friendly," Meyer said.

"It's just we don't like hustlers."

"I got your message three times already," Meyer said. "Eight ball in the side." He shot and missed.

"Where'd you learn to shoot pool?" Tino said.

"My father taught me."

"Was he as lousy as you?"

Meyer didn't answer.

"What's that in your belt there?"

"That's a hook," Meyer said.

"What's it for?"

"I use it," Meyer said.

"You work on the docks?"

"That's right."

"Where?"

"On the docks," Meyer said.

"Yeah, *where* on the docks?"

"Look, friend," Meyer said, and put down the pool cue and stared at Tino.

"Yeah?"

"What's it your business where I work?"

"I like to know who comes in here."

"Why? You own the joint?"

"My brother does."

"Okay," Meyer said, "My name's Stu Levine, I'm working the Leary Street docks right now, unloading the S.S. *Agda* out of Sweden. I live downtown on Ridgeway, and I happened to notice there was a pool hall here, so I decided to come in and run off a few racks before heading home. You think that'll satisfy your brother, or do you want to see my birth certificate?"

"You Jewish?" Tino asked.

"Funny I don't look it, right?"

"No, you *do* look it."

"So?"

"So nothing. We get some Jewish guys from around the corner in here every now and then."

"I'm glad to hear it. Is it okay to shoot now?"

"You want company?"

"How do I know *you're* not a hustler?"

"We'll pay for time, how's that?"

"You'll win," Meyer said.

"So what? It's better than playing alone, ain't it?"

"I came up here to shoot a few balls and enjoy myself," Meyer said. "Why should I play with somebody better than me? I'll get stuck with the time, and you'll be doing all the shooting."

"You could consider it a lesson."

"I don't need lessons."

"You need lessons, believe me," Tino said. "The way you shoot pool, it's a disgrace."

"If I need lessons, I'll get Minnesota Fats."

"There ain't no real person named Minnesota Fats," Tino said, "he was just a guy they made up," which reminded Meyer that someone had named a fictitious character after him, and which further reminded him that he had not yet heard from Rollie Chabrier down at the D.A.'s office.

"Looks like I'll never get to shoot, anyway," he said, "if you're gonna stand here and gab all day."

"Okay?" Tino said.

"Go ahead, take a cue," Meyer said, and sighed. He felt he had handled the encounter very well. He had not seemed too anxious to be friendly, and yet he had succeeded in promoting a game with one of the pool hall regulars. When La Bresca walked in, if indeed he ever did, he would find Tino playing with his good old buddy Stu Levine from the Leary Street docks. Very good, Meyer thought, they ought to up me a grade tomorrow morning.

"First off, you hold your cue wrong," Tino said. "Here's how you got to hold it if you expect to sink anything."

"Like this?" Meyer said, trying to imitate the grip.

"You got arthritis or something?" Tino asked, and burst out laughing at his own joke, proving to Meyer's satisfaction that he really did not have a sense of humor.

Tino was demonstrating the proper English to put on the cue ball in order to have it veer to the left after contact, and Meyer was alternately watching the clock and the door when La Bresca walked in some twenty minutes later. Meyer recognized him at once from the description he'd been given, but turned away immediately, not wanting to seem at all interested, and listened to Tino's explanation, and then listened to the meager joke Tino offered, something about the reason it's called English is because if you hit an Englishman in the balls with a stick, they'll turn white just like the cue ball on the table, get it? Tino laughed, and Meyer laughed with him, and that was what La Bresca saw as he approached the table, Tino and his good old buddy from the Leary Street docks, laughing it up and shooting a friendly game of pool in the friendly neighborhood pool hall.

"Hi, Tino," La Bresca said.

"Hi, Tony."

"How's it going?"

"So-so. This here is Stu Levine."

"Glad to meet you," La Bresca said.

"Same here," Meyer said, and extended his hand.

"This here is Tony La Bresca. He shoots a good game."

"Nobody shoots as good as you," La Bresca said.

"Stu here shoots the way Angie used to. You remember Angie who was crippled? That's the way Stu here shoots."

"Yeah, I remember Angie," La Bresca said, and both men burst out laughing. Meyer laughed with them, what the hell.

"Stu's father taught him," Tino said.

"Yeah? Who taught his father?" La Bresca said, and both men burst out laughing again.

"I hear you got yourself a job," Tino said.

"That's right."

"You just getting through?"

"Yeah, I thought I'd shoot a game or two before supper. You see Calooch around?"

"Yeah, he's over there by the windows."

"Thought maybe I'd shoot a game with him."

"Why'nt you join us right here?" Tino said.

"Thanks," La Bresca said, "but I promised Calooch I'd shoot a game with him. Anyway, you're too much of a shark."

"A shark, you hear that, Stu?" Tino said. "He thinks I'm a shark."

"Well, I'll see you," La Bresca said, and walked over to the window table. A tall thin man in a striped shirt was bent over the table, angling for a shot. La Bresca waited until he had run off three or four balls, and then they both went up to the front booth. The lights suddenly came on over a table across the hall. La Bresca and the man named Calooch went to the table, took sticks down, racked up the balls, and began playing.

"Who's Calooch?" Meyer asked Tino.

"Oh, that's Pete Calucci," Tino said.

"Friend of Tony's?"

"Oh, yeah, they know each other a long time."

Calooch and La Bresca were doing a lot of talking. They weren't doing too much playing, but they sure were talking a lot. They talked, and then one of them took a shot, and then they talked some more, and after a while the other one took a shot, and it went like that for almost an hour. At the end of the hour, both men put up

their sticks, and shook hands. Calooch went back to the
window table, and La Bresca went up front to settle for
the time. Meyer looked up at the clock and said, "Wow,
look at that, already six o'clock. I better get home, my
wife'll murder me."

"Well, Stu, I enjoyed playing with you," Tino said.
"Stop in again sometime."

"Yeah, maybe I will," Meyer said.

The street outside was caught in the pale gray grasp
of dusk, empty, silent except for the keening of the wind,
bitterly cold, forbidding. Anthony La Bresca walked
with his hands in the pockets of his beige car coat, the
collar raised, the green muffler wound about his neck
and flapping in the fierce wind. Meyer stayed far behind
him, mindful of Kling's embarrassing encounter the
night before and determined not to have the same thing
happen to an old experienced workhorse like himself.
The cold weather and the resultant empty streets did not
help him very much. It was comparatively simple to tail
a man on a crowded street, but when there are only two
people left alive in the world, the one up front might
suddenly turn at the sound of a footfall or a tail-of-the-
eye glimpse of something or someone behind him. So
Meyer kept his distance and utilized every doorway he
could find, ducking in and out of the street, grateful for
the frantic activity that helped ward off the cold, convinced he would not be spotted, but mindful of the alter-
nate risk he was running: if La Bresca turned a corner
suddenly, or entered a building unexpectedly, Meyer
could very well lose him.

The girl was waiting in a Buick.

The car was black, Meyer made the year and make at once, but he could not read the license plate because the car was too far away, parked at the curb some two blocks up the street. The engine was running. The exhaust threw gray plumes of carbon monoxide into the gray and empty street. La Bresca stopped at the car, and Meyer ducked into the closest doorway, the windowed alcove of a pawnshop. Surrounded by saxophones and typewriters, cameras and tennis rackets, fishing rods and loving cups, Meyer looked diagonally through the joined and angled windows of the shop and squinted his eyes in an attempt to read the license plate of the Buick. He could not make out the numbers. The girl had blond hair, it fell loose to the base of her neck, she leaned over on the front seat to open the door for La Bresca.

La Bresca got into the car and slammed the door behind him.

Meyer came out of the doorway just as the big black Buick gunned away from the curb.

He still could not read the license plate.

7

NOBODY LIKES TO WORK ON SATURDAY.

There's something obscene about it, it goes against the human grain. Saturday is the day before the day of rest, a good time to stomp on all those pressures that have been building Monday to Friday. Given a nice blustery rotten March day with the promise of snow in the air and the city standing expectantly monolithic, stoic, and solemn, given such a peach of a Saturday, how nice to be able to start a cannel coal fire in the fireplace of your three-room apartment and smoke yourself out of the joint. Or, lacking a fireplace, what better way to utilize Saturday than by pouring yourself a stiff hooker of bourbon and curling up with a blonde or a book, spending your time with *War and Peace* or *Whore and Piece*, didn't Shakespeare invent some of his best puns on Saturday, drunk with a wench in his first best bed?

Saturday is quiet day. It can drive you to distraction

with its prospects of leisure time, it can force you to pick at the coverlet wondering what to do with all your sudden freedom, it can send you wandering through the rooms in search of occupation while moodily contemplating the knowledge that the loneliest night of the week is fast approaching.

Nobody likes to work on Saturday because nobody else is working on Saturday.

Except cops.

Grind, grind, grind, work, work, work, driven by a sense of public-mindedness and dedication to humanity, law enforcement officers are forever at the ready, alert of mind, swift of body, noble of purpose.

Andy Parker was asleep in the swivel chair behind his desk.

"Where is everybody?" one of the painters said.

"What?" Parker said. "Huh?" Parker said, and sat bolt upright, and glared at the painter and then washed his huge hand over his face and said, "What the hell's the matter with you, scaring a man that way?"

"We're leaving," the first painter said.

"We're finished," the second painter said.

"We already got all our gear loaded on the truck, and we wanted to say good-by to everybody."

"So where is everybody?"

"There's a meeting in the lieutenant's office," Parker said.

"We'll just pop in and say good-by," the first painter said.

"I wouldn't advise that," Parker said.

"Why not?"

"They're discussing homicide. It's not wise to pop in on people when they're discussing homicide."

"Not even to say good-by?"

"You can say good-by to *me*," Parker said.

"It wouldn't be the same thing," the first painter said.

"So then hang around and say good-by when they come out. They should be finished before twelve. In fact, they *got* to be finished before twelve."

"Yeah, but *we're* finished *now*," the second painter said.

"Can't you find a few things you missed?" Parker suggested. "Like, for example, you didn't paint the type-writers, or the bottle on the water cooler, or our guns. How come you missed our guns? You got green all over everything else in the goddamn place."

"You should be grateful," the first painter said. "Some people won't work on Saturday *at all*, even at time and a half."

So both painters left in high dudgeon, and Parker went back to sleep in the swivel chair behind his desk.

"I don't know what kind of a squad I'm running here," Lieutenant Byrnes said, "when two experienced detectives can blow a surveillance, one by getting made first crack out of the box, and the other by losing his man; that's a pretty good batting average for two experienced detectives."

"I was told the suspect didn't have a car." Meyer said. "I was told he had taken a train the night before."

"That's right, he did," Kling said.

"I had no way of knowing a woman would be waiting for him in a car," Meyer said.

"So you lost him," Byrnes said, "which might have been all right if the man had gone home last night. But O'Brien was stationed outside the La Bresca house in Riverhead, and the man never showed, which means we don't know where he is today, now do we? We don't know where a prime suspect is on the day the deputy mayor is supposed to get killed."

"No, sir," Meyer said, "we don't know where La Bresca is."

"Because *you* lost him."

"I guess so, sir."

"Well, how would you revise that statement, Meyer?"

"I wouldn't, sir. I lost him."

"Yes, very good, I'll put you in for a commendation."

"Thank you, sir."

"Don't get flip, Meyer."

"I'm sorry, sir."

"This isn't a goddamn joke here, I don't want Scanlon to wind up with two holes in his head the way Cowper did."

"No, sir, neither do I."

"Okay, then learn for Christ's sake how to tail a person, will you?"

"Yes, sir."

"Now what about this other man you say La Bresca spent time with in conversation, what was his name?"

"Calucci, sir. Peter Calucci."

"Did you check him out?"

"Yes, sir, last night before I went home. Here's the stuff we got from the B.C.I."

Meyer placed a manila envelope on Byrnes' desk, and then stepped back to join the other detectives ranged in a military line before the desk. None of the men was smiling. The lieutenant was in a lousy mood, and somebody was supposed to come up with fifty thousand dollars before noon, and the possibility existed that the deputy mayor would soon be dispatched to that big City Hall in the sky, so nobody was smiling. The lieutenant reached into the envelope and pulled out a photocopy of a fingerprint card, glanced at it cursorily, and then pulled out a photocopy of Calucci's police record.

Byrnes read the sheet, and then said, "When did he get out?"

"He was a bad apple. He applied for parole after serving a third of the sentence, was denied, and applied every year after that. He finally made it in seven."

Byrnes looked at the sheet again.

IDENTIFICATION BUREAU

NAME ___Peter Vincent Calucci_____

IDENTIFICATION JACKET NUMBER ___P 421904_____

ALIAS _____"Calooch"   "Cooch"   "Kook"_____

_____ COLOR __White____

RESIDENCE ___336 South 91st Street, Isola_____

DATE OF BIRTH ___October 2, 1938_____ AGE __22___

BIRTHPLACE ___Isola_____

HEIGHT ___5'9"___ WEIGHT ___156___ HAIR _Brown_ EYES _Brown_

COMPLEXION _Swarthy____ OCCUPATION _Construction worker_

SCARS AND TATTOOS ___Appendectomy scar, no tattoos.___

ARRESTED BY: ___Patrolman Henry Butler_____

DETECTIVE DIVISION NUMBER: ___63-R1-1605-1960_____

DATE OF ARREST _3/14/60_____ PLACE _812 North 65 St., Isola_

CHARGE ___Robbery_____

BRIEF DETAILS OF CRIME _Calucci entered gasoline station at_
___812 North 65 Street at or about midnight, threatened_
___to shoot attendant if he did not open safe. Attendant_
___said he did not know combination, Calucci cocked_
___revolver and was about to fire when patrolman Butler_
___of 63rd Precinct came upon scene and apprehended him._

PREVIOUS RECORD ___None_____

INDICTED . ___Criminal Courts, March 15, 1960._____

FINAL CHARGE ___Robbery in first degree, Penal Law 2125___

DISPOSITION ___Pleaded guilty 7/8/60, sentenced to ten_
_____years at Castleview Prison._____

"What's he been doing?" Byrnes asked.

"Construction work."

"That how he met La Bresca?"

"Calucci's parole officer reports that his last job was with Abco Construction, and a call to the company listed La Bresca as having worked there at the same time."

"I forget, does this La Bresca have a record?"

"No, sir."

"Has Calucci been clean since he got out?"

"According to his parole officer, yes, sir."

"Now who's this person 'Dom' who called La Bresca Thursday night?"

"We have no idea, sir."

"Because La Bresca tipped to your tailing him, isn't that right, Kling?"

"Yes, sir, that's right, sir."

"Is Brown still on that phone tap?"

"Yes, sir."

"Have you tried any of our stoolies?"

"No, sir, not yet."

"Well, when the hell do you propose to get moving? We're supposed to deliver fifty thousand dollars by twelve o'clock. It's now a quarter after ten, when the hell . . ."

"Sir, we've been trying to get a line on Calucci. His parole officer gave us an address, and we sent a man over, but his landlady says he hasn't been there since early yesterday morning."

"Of course not!" Byrnes shouted. "The two of them are probably shacked up with that blond woman, whoever the hell *she* was, planning how to murder Scanlon when we fail to deliver the payoff money. Get Danny Gimp or Fats Donner, find out if they know a fellow named Dom who dropped a bundle on a big fight two weeks ago. Who the hell was fighting two weeks ago, anyway? Was that the championship fight?"

"Yes, sir."

"All right, get cracking. Does anybody use Gimp besides Carella?"

"No, sir."

"Who uses Donner?"

"I do, sir."

"Then get him right away, Willis."

"If he's not in Florida, sir. He usually goes south in the winter."

"Goddamn stool pigeons go south," Byrnes grumbled, "and we're stuck here with a bunch of maniacs trying to kill people. All right, go on, Willis, get moving."

"Yes, sir," Willis said, and left the office.

"Now what about this other possibility, this deaf man thing? Jesus Christ, I hope it's not him, I hope this is La Bresca and Calucci and the blond bimbo who drove him clear out of sight last night, Meyer . . ."

"Yes, sir . . ."

". . . and not that deaf bastard again. I've talked to the commissioner on this, and I've also talked to the deputy mayor *and* the mayor, and we're agreed that paying the fifty thousand dollars is out of the question. We're to try apprehending whoever picks up that lunch pail and see if we can't get a lead this time. And we're to provide protection for Scanlon and that's all for now. So I want you two to arrange the drop, and saturation coverage of that bench, and I want a suspect brought in here today, and I want him questioned till he's blue in the face, have a lawyer ready and waiting for him in case he screams Miranda-Escobedo, I want a *lead* today, have you got that?"

"Yes, sir," Meyer said.

"Yes, sir," Kling said.

"You think you can set up the drop and cover without fouling it up like you fouled up the surveillance?"

"Yes, sir, we can handle it."

"All right, then get going, and bring me some meat on this goddamn case."

"Yes, sir," Kling and Meyer said together, and then went out of the office.

"Now what's this about a junkie being in that room with the killer?" Byrnes asked Hawes.

"That's right, sir."

"Well, what's your idea, Cotton?"

"My idea is he got her in there to make sure she'd be stoned when he started shooting, that's my idea, sir."

"That's the stupidest idea I've ever heard in my life," Byrnes said. "Get the hell out of here, go help Meyer and Kling, go call the hospital, find out how Carella's doing, go set up another plant for those two punks who beat him up, go do *something*, for Christ's sake!"

"Yes, sir," Hawes said, and went out into the squad-room.

Andy Parker, awakened by the grumbling of the other men, washed his hand over his face, blew his nose, and then said, "The painters said to tell you good-by."

"Good riddance," Meyer said.

"Also, you got a call from the D.A.'s office."

"Who from?"

"Rollie Chabrier."

"When was this?"

"Half-hour ago, I guess."

"Why didn't you put it through?"

"While you were in there with the loot? No, sir."

"I've been waiting for this call," Meyer said, and immediately dialed Chabrier's number.

"Mr. Chabrier's office," a bright female voice said.

"Bernice, this is Meyer Meyer up at the 87th. I hear Rollie called me a little while ago."

"That's right," Bernice said.

"Would you put him on, please?"

"He's gone for the day," Bernice said.

"Gone for the day? It's only a little after ten."

"Well," Bernice said, "nobody likes to work on Saturday."

The black lunch pail containing approximately fifty thousand scraps of newspaper was placed in the center of the third bench on the Clinton Street footpath into Grover Park by Detective Cotton Hawes, who was wearing thermal underwear and two sweaters and a business suit and an overcoat and ear muffs. Hawes was an expert skier, and he had skied on days when the temperature at the base was four below zero and the temperature at the summit was thirty below, had skied on days when his feet went and his hands went and he boomed the mountain non-stop not for fun or sport but just to get near the fire in the base lodge before he shattered into a hundred brittle pieces. But he had never been this cold before. It was bad enough to be working on Saturday, but it was indecent to be working when the weather threatened to gelatinize a man's blood.

Among the other people who were braving the unseasonable winds and temperatures that Saturday were:

(1) A pretzel salesman at the entrance to the Clinton Street footpath.

(2) Two nuns saying their beads on the second bench into the park.

(3) A passionate couple necking in a sleeping bag on the grass behind the third bench.

(4) A blind man sitting on the fourth bench, patting his seeing eye German shepherd and scattering bread crumbs to the pigeons.

The pretzel salesman was a detective named Stanley Faulk, recruited from the 88th across the park, a man of fifty-eight who wore a gray handlebar mustache as his trademark. The mustache made it quite simple to identify him when he was working in his own territory, thereby diminishing his value on plants. But it also served to strike terror into the hearts of hoods near and wide, in much the same way that the green-and-white color combination of a radio motor patrol car is supposed to frighten criminals and serve as a deterrent. Faulk wasn't too happy about being called into service for the 87th on a day like this one, but he was bundled up warmly in several sweaters over which was a black cardigan-type candy store-owner sweater over which he had put on a white apron. He was standing behind a cart that displayed pretzels stacked on long round sticks. A walkie-talkie was set into the top of the cart.

The two nuns saying their beads were Detectives Meyer Meyer and Bert Kling, and they were really saying what a son of a bitch Byrnes had been to bawl them out that way in front of Hawes and Willis, embarrassing them and making them feel very foolish.

"I feel very foolish right now," Meyer whispered.

"How come?" Kling whispered.

"I feel like I'm in drag," Meyer whispered.

The passionate couple assignment had been the choice assignment, and Hawes and Willis had drawn straws for it. The reason it was so choice was that the other half of the passionate couple was herself quite choice, a policewoman named Eileen Burke, with whom Willis had worked on a mugging case many years back. Eileen had red hair and green eyes, Eileen had long legs, sleek and clean, full-calved, tapering to slender ankles, Eileen had very good breasts, and whereas Eileen was much taller than Willis (who only barely scraped past the five-foot-eight height requirement), he did not mind at all because big girls always seemed attracted to him, and vice versa.

"We're supposed to be kissing," he said to Eileen, and held her close in the warm sleeping bag.

"My lips are getting chapped," she said.

"Your lips are very nice," he said.

"We're supposed to be here on business," Eileen said.

"Mmm," he answered.

"Get your hand off my behind," she said.

"Oh, is that your behind?" he asked.

"Listen," she said.

"I hear it," he said. "Somebody's coming. You'd better kiss me."

She kissed him. Willis kept one eye on the bench. The person passing was a governess wheeling a baby carriage, God knew who would send an infant out on a day when the glacier was moving south. The woman and the carriage passed. Willis kept kissing Detective 2nd/Grade Eileen Burke.

"Mm frick sheb brom," Eileen mumbled.

"Mmm?" Willis mumbled.

Eileen pulled her mouth away and caught her breath. "I *said* I think she's gone."

"What's that?" Willis asked suddenly.

"Do not be afraid, *guapa*, it is only my pistol," Eileen said, and laughed.

"I meant on the path. Listen."

They listened.

Someone else was approaching the bench.

From where Patrolman Richard Genero sat in plain-clothes on the fourth bench, wearing dark glasses and patting the head of the German shepherd at his feet, tossing crumbs to the pigeons, wishing for summer, he could clearly see the young man who walked rapidly to the third bench, picked up the lunch pail, looked swiftly over his shoulder, and began walking not *out* of the park, but deeper *into* it.

Genero didn't know quite what to do at first.

He had been pressed into duty only because there was a shortage of available men that afternoon (crime prevention being an arduous and difficult task on any given day, but especially on Saturday), and he had been placed in the position thought least vulnerable, it being assumed the man who picked up the lunch pail would immediately reverse direction and head out of the park again, onto Grover Avenue, where Faulk the pretzel man and Hawes, parked in his own car at the curb, would immediately collar him. But the suspect was coming into the park instead, heading for Genero's bench, and Genero was a fellow who didn't care very much for violence, so he sat there wishing he was home in bed, with his mother serving him hot *minestrone* and singing old Italian arias.

The dog at his feet had been trained for police work, and Genero had been taught a few hand signals and voice signals in the squadroom before heading out for this vigil on the fourth bench, but he was also afraid of dogs, especially big dogs, and the idea of giving this animal a kill command that might possibly be misunderstood filled Genero with fear and trembling. Suppose he gave the command and the dog leaped for his *own* jugular rather than for the throat of the young man who was perhaps three feet away now and walking quite rapidly, glancing over his shoulder every now and again? Suppose he did that and this beast tore him to shreds, what would his mother say to that? *che bella cosa*, you hadda to become a police, hah?

Willis, in the meantime, had slid his walkie-talkie up between Eileen Burke's breasts and flashed the news to Hawes, parked in his own car on Grover Avenue, good place to be when your man is going the other way. Willis was now desperately trying to lower the zipper on the bag, which zipper seemed to have become somehow stuck. Willis didn't mind being stuck in a sleeping bag with someone like Eileen Burke, who wiggled and wriggled along with him as they attempted to extricate themselves, but he suddenly fantasied the lieutenant chewing him out the way he had chewed out Kling and Meyer this morning and so he really *was* trying to lower that damn zipper while entertaining the further fantasy that Eileen Burke was beginning to enjoy all this adolescent tumbling. Genero, of course, didn't know that Hawes had been alerted, he only knew that the suspect was abreast of him now, and passing the bench now, and moving swiftly beyond the bench now, so he got up and first took off the sun-glasses, and then unbuttoned the third button of his coat the way he had seen detectives do on television, and then reached in for his revolver and then shot himself in the leg.

The suspect began running.

Genero fell to the ground and the dog licked his face.

Willis got out of the sleeping bag and Eileen Burke buttoned her blouse and her coat and then adjusted her garters, and Hawes came running into the park and slipped on a patch of ice near the third bench and almost broke his neck.

"Stop, police!" Willis shouted.

And, miracle of miracles, the suspect stopped dead in his tracks and waited for Willis to approach him with his gun in his hand and lipstick all over his face.

The suspect's name was Alan Parry.

They advised him of his rights and he agreed to talk to them without a lawyer, even though a lawyer was present and waiting for him in case he demanded one.

"Where do you live, Alan?" Willis asked.

"Right around the corner. I know you guys. I see you guys around all the time. Don't you know me? I live right around the corner."

"You make him?" Willis asked the other detectives.

They all shook their heads. They were standing around him in a loose circle, the pretzel man, two nuns, the pair of lovers and the big redhead with a white streak in his hair and a throbbing ankle in his thermal underwear.

"Why'd you run, Alan?" Willis asked.

"I heard a shot. In this neighborhood, when you hear shooting, you run."

"Who's your partner?"

"What partner?"

"The guy who's in this with you."

"In *what* with me?"

"The murder plot."

"The *what*?"

"Come on, Alan, you play ball with us, we'll play ball with you."

"Hey, man, you got the wrong customer," Parry said.

"How were you going to split the loot, Alan?"

"What loot?"

"The loot in that lunch pail."

"Listen, I never seen that lunch pail before in my life."

"There's thirty thousand dollars in that lunch pail,"

Willis said, "now come on, Alan, you know that, stop playing it cozy."

Parry either avoided the trap, or else did not know there was supposed to be *fifty* thousand dollars in the black pail he had lifted from the bench. He shook his head and said, "I don't know nothing about no loot, I was asked to pick up the pail, and I done it."

"Who asked you?"

"A big blond guy wearing a hearing aid."

"Do you expect me to believe that?" Willis said.

The cue was one the detectives of the 87th had used many times before in interrogating suspects, and it was immediately seized upon by Meyer, who said, "Take it easy, Hal," the proper response, the response that told Willis they were once again ready to assume antagonistic roles. In the charade that would follow, Willis would play the tough bastard out to hang a phony rap on poor little Alan Parry, while Meyer would play the sympathetic father figure. The other detectives (including Faulk of the 88th, who was familiar with the ploy and had used it often enough himself in his own squadroom) would serve as a sort of nodding Greek chorus, impartial and objective.

Without even so much as a glance at Meyer, Willis said, "What do you mean, take it easy? This little punk has been lying from the minute we got him up here."

"Maybe there really *was* a tall blond guy with a hearing aid," Meyer said. "Give him a chance to tell us, will you?"

"Sure, and maybe there was a striped elephant with pink polka dots," Willis said. "Who's your partner, you little punk?"

"I don't *have* no partner!" Parry said. Plaintively, he said to Meyer, "Will you please tell this guy I ain't *got* a partner?"

"Calm down, Hal, will you?" Meyer said. "Let's hear it, Alan."

"I was on my way home when . . ."

"From where?" Willis snapped.

"Huh?"

"Where were you coming from?"

"From my girl's house."

"Where?"

"Around the corner. Right across the street from my house."

"What were you doing there?"

"Well, you know," Parry said.

"No, we *don't* know," Willis said.

"For God's sake, Hal," Meyer said, "leave the man a little something personal and private, will you please?"

"Thanks," Parry said.

"You went to see your girl friend," Meyer said. "What time was that, Alan?"

"I went up there around nine-thirty. Her mother goes to work at nine. So I went up around nine-thirty."

"You unemployed?" Willis snapped.

"Yes, sir," Parry said.

"When's the last time you worked?"

"Well, you see . . ."

"Answer the question!"

"Give him a chance, Hal!"

"He's stalling!"

"He's trying to answer you!" Gently, Meyer said, "What happened, Alan?"

"I had this job, and I dropped the eggs."

"What?"

"At the grocery store on Eightieth. I was working in the back and one day we got all these crates of eggs, and I was taking them to the refrigerator, and I dropped two crates. So I got fired."

"How long did you work there?"

"From when I got out of high school."

"When was that?" Willis asked.

"Last June."

"Did you graduate?"

"Yes, sir, I have a diploma," Parry said.

"So what have you been doing since you lost the job at the grocery?"

Parry shrugged. "Nothing," he said.

"How old are you?" Willis asked.

"I'll be nineteen . . . what's today?"

"Today's the ninth."

"I'll be nineteen next week. The fifteenth of March."

"You're liable to be spending your birthday in jail," Willis said.

"Now cut it out," Meyer said, "I won't have you threatening this man. What happened when you left your girl friend's house, Alan?"

"I met this guy."

"Where?"

"Outside the Corona."

"The what?"

"The Corona. You know the movie house that's all

boarded up about three blocks from here, you know the one?"

"We know it," Willis said.

"Well, there."

"What was he doing there?"

"Just standing. Like as if he was waiting for somebody."

"So what happened?"

"He stopped me and said was I busy? So I said it depended. So he said would I like to make five bucks? So I asked him doing what? He said there was a lunch pail in the park, and if I picked it up for him, he'd give me five bucks. So I asked him why he couldn't go for it himself, and he said he was waiting there for somebody, and he was afraid if he left the guy might show up and think he'd gone. So he said I should get the lunch pail for him and bring it back to him there outside the theater so he wouldn't miss his friend. He was supposed to meet him outside the Corona, you see. You know the place? A cop got shot outside there once."

"I told you we know it," Willis said.

"So I asked him what was in the lunch pail, and he said just his lunch, so I said he could buy *some* lunch for five bucks, but he said he also had a few other things in there with his sandwiches, so I asked him like what and he said do you want this five bucks or not? So I took the five and went to get the pail for him."

"He gave you the five dollars?"

"Yeah."

"*Before* you went for the pail?"

"Yeah."

"Go on."

"He's lying," Willis said.

"This is the truth, I swear to God."

"What'd you think was in that pail?"

Parry shrugged. "Lunch. And some other little things. Like he said."

"Come on," Willis said, "do you expect us to buy that?"

"Kid, what'd you *really* think was in that pail?" Meyer asked gently.

"Well . . . look . . . you can't do nothing to me for what I *thought* was in there, right?"

"That's right," Meyer said. "If you could lock up a man for what he's thinking, we'd *all* be in jail, right?"

"Right," Parry said, and laughed.

Meyer laughed with him. The Greek chorus laughed too. Everybody laughed except Willis, who kept staring stone-faced at Parry. "So what'd you *think* was in the pail?" Meyer said.

"Junk," Parry said.

"You a junkie?" Willis asked.

"No, sir, never touch the stuff."

"Roll up your sleeve."

"I'm not a junkie, sir."

"Let's see your arm."

Parry rolled up his sleeve.

"Okay," Willis said.

"I told you," Parry said.

"Okay, you told us. What'd you plan to do with that lunch pail?"

"What do you mean?"

"The Corona is three blocks east of there. You picked up that pail and started heading west. What were you planning?"

"Nothing."

"Then why were you heading *away* from where the deaf man was waiting?"

"I wasn't heading anyplace."

"You were heading *west*."

"No. I musta got mixed up."

"You got so mixed up you forgot how you came into the park, right? You forgot that the entrance was *behind* you, right?"

"No, I didn't forget where the entrance was."

"Then why'd you head deeper into the park?"

"I told you. I musta got mixed up."

"He's a lying little bastard," Willis said. "I'm going to book him, Meyer, no matter *what* you say."

"Now hold it, just hold it a minute," Meyer said. "You know you're in pretty serious trouble if there's junk in that pail, don't you, Alan?" Meyer said.

"Why? Even if there *is* junk in there, it ain't mine."

"Well, *I* know that, Alan, *I* believe you, but the law is pretty specific about possession of narcotics. I'm sure you must realize that every pusher we pick up claims somebody must have planted the stuff on him, he doesn't know how it got there, it isn't his, and so on. They all give the same excuses, even when we've got them dead to rights."

"Yeah, I guess they must," Parry said.

"So you see, I won't be able to help you much if there really *is* junk in that pail."

"Yeah, I see," Parry said.

"He knows there's no junk in that pail. His partner sent him to pick up the money," Willis said.

"No, no," Parry said, shaking his head.

"You didn't know anything about the thirty thousand dollars, is that right?" Meyer asked gently.

"Nothing," Parry said, shaking his head. "I'm telling you, I met this guy outside the Corona and he gave me five bucks to go get his pail."

"Which you decided to steal," Willis said.

"Huh?"

"Were you going to bring that pail back to him?"

"Well . . ." Parry hesitated. He glanced at Meyer. Meyer nodded encouragingly. "Well, no," Parry said. "I figured if there was junk in it, maybe I could turn a quick buck, you know. There's lots of guys in this neighborhood'll pay for stuff like that."

"Stuff like what?" Willis asked.

"Like what's in the pail," Parry said.

"Open the pail, kid," Willis said.

"No." Parry shook his head. "No, I don't want to."

"Why not?"

"If it's junk, I don't know nothing about it. And if it's thirty G's, I got nothing to do with it. I don't know nothing. I don't want to answer no more questions, that's it."

"That's it, Hal," Meyer said.

"Go on home, kid," Willis said.

"I can go?"

"Yeah, yeah, you can go," Willis said wearily.

Parry stood up quickly, and without looking back

headed straight for the gate in the slatted railing that divided the squadroom from the corridor outside. He was down the hallway in a wink. His footfalls clattered noisily on the iron-runged steps leading to the street floor below.

"What do you think?" Willis said.

"I think we did it ass-backwards," Hawes said. "I think we should have followed him out of the park instead of nailing him. He would have led us straight to the deaf man."

"The lieutenant didn't think so. The lieutenant figured nobody would be crazy enough to send a stranger after fifty thousand dollars. The lieutenant figured the guy who made the pickup *had* to be a member of the gang."

"Yeah, well the lieutenant was wrong," Hawes said.

"You know what I think?" Kling said.

"What?"

"I think the deaf man *knew* there'd be nothing in that lunch pail. That's why he could risk sending a stranger for it. He *knew* the money wouldn't be there, and he *knew* we'd pick up whoever he sent."

"If that's the case . . ." Willis started.

"He *wants* to kill Scanlon," Kling said.

The detectives all looked at each other. Faulk scratched his head and said, "Well, I better be getting back across the park, unless you need me some more."

"No, thanks a lot, Stan," Meyer said.

"Don't mention it." Faulk said, and went out.

"I enjoyed the plant," Eileen Burke said, and glanced

archly at Willis, and then swiveled toward the gate and out of the squadroom.

"Can it be the breeze . . ." Meyer sang.

"That fills the trees . . ." Kling joined in.

"Go to hell," Willis said, and then genuflected and piously added, "Sisters."

If nobody in the entire world likes working on Saturday, even less people like working on Saturday night.

Saturday night, baby, is the night to howl. Saturday night is the night to get out there and hang ten. Saturday night is when you slip into your satin slippers and your Pucci dress, put on your shirt with the monogram on the cuff, spray your navel with cologne, and laugh too loud.

The bitch city is something different on Saturday night, sophisticated in black, scented and powdered, but somehow not as unassailable, shiveringly beautiful in a dazzle of blinking lights. Reds and oranges, electric blues and vibrant greens assault the eye incessantly, and the resultant turn-on is as sweet as a quick sharp fix in a penthouse pad, a liquid cool that conjures dreams of towering glass spires and enameled minarets. There is excitement in this city on Saturday night, but it is tempered by romantic expectancy. She is not a bitch, this city. Not on Saturday night.

Not if you will love her.

Nobody likes to work on Saturday night, and so the detectives of the 87th Squad should have been pleased when the police commissioner called Byrnes to say that he was asking the D.A.'s Squad to assume the responsibility of protecting Deputy Mayor Scanlon from harm. If they'd had any sense at all, the detectives of the 87th would have considered themselves fortunate.

But the commissioner's cut was deeply felt, first by Byrnes, and then by every man on the squad when he related the news to them. They went their separate ways that Saturday night, some into the streets to work, others home to rest, but each of them felt a corporate sense of failure. Not one of them realized how fortunate he was.

The two detectives from the D.A.'s Squad were experienced men who had handled special assignments before. When the deputy mayor's personal chauffeur arrived to pick them up that night, they were waiting on the sidewalk outside the Criminal Courts Building, just around the corner from the District Attorney's office. It was exactly 8:00 P.M. The deputy mayor's chauffeur had picked up the Cadillac sedan at the municipal garage a half-hour earlier. He had gone over the upholstery with a whisk broom, passed a dust rag over the hood, wiped the windows with a chamois cloth, and emptied all the ashtrays. He was now ready for action, and he was pleased to note that the detectives were right on time; he could not abide tardy individuals.

They drove up to Smoke Rise, which was where the deputy mayor lived, and one of the detectives got out of the car and walked to the front door, and rang the bell, and was ushered into the huge brick house by a maid in a black uniform. The deputy mayor came down the long white staircase leading to the center hall, shook hands with the detective from the D.A.'s Squad, apologized for taking up his time this way on a Saturday night, made some comment about the "damn foolishness of it all," and then called up to his wife to tell her the car was waiting. His wife came down the steps, and the deputy mayor introduced her to the detective from the D.A.'s Squad, and then they all went to the front door.

The detective stepped outside first, scanned the bushes lining the driveway, and then led the deputy mayor and his wife to the car. He opened the door and allowed them to precede him into the automobile. The other detective was stationed on the opposite side of the car, and as soon as the deputy mayor and his wife were seated, both detectives got into the automobile and took positions facing them on the jump seats.

The dashboard clock read 8:30 P.M.

The deputy mayor's personal chauffeur set the car in motion, and the deputy mayor made a few jokes with the detectives as they drove along the gently winding roads of exclusive Smoke Rise on the edge of the city's northern river, and then onto the service road leading to the River Highway. It had been announced in the newspapers the week before that the deputy mayor would speak at a meeting of the B'nai Brith in the city's largest synagogue at nine o'clock that night. The deputy mayor's home in Smoke Rise was only fifteen minutes away from the synagogue, and so the chauffeur drove slowly and carefully while the two detectives from the D.A.'s Squad eyed the automobiles that moved past on either side of the Cadillac.

The Cadillac exploded when the dashboard clock read 8:45 P.M.

The bomb was a powerful one.

It erupted from somewhere under the hood, sending

flying steel into the car, tearing off the roof like paper, blowing the doors into the highway. The car screeched out of control, lurched across two lanes, rolled onto its side like a ruptured metal beast and was suddenly ablaze.

A passing convertible tried to swerve around the flaming Cadillac. There was a second explosion. The convertible veered wildly and crashed into the river barrier.

When the police arrived on the scene, the only person alive in either car was a bleeding seventeen-year-old girl who had gone through the windshield of the convertible.

8

On Sunday morning, the visiting hours at Buena Vista Hospital were from ten to twelve. It was a busy day, busier than Wednesday, for example, because Saturday night encourages broken arms and legs, bloody pates and shattered sternums. There is nothing quite so hectic as the Emergency Room of a big city hospital on a Saturday night. And on Sunday morning it's only natural for people to visit the friends and relatives who were unfortunate enough to have met with assorted mayhem the night before.

Steve Carella had met with assorted mayhem on Thursday night, and here it was Sunday morning, and he sat propped up in bed expecting Teddy's arrival and feeling gaunt and pale and unshaven even though he had shaved himself not ten minutes ago. He had lost seven pounds since his admission to the hospital (it being singularly difficult to eat and breathe at the same time when your nose is taped and bandaged) and he still ached everywhere, seemed in fact to discover new bruises every time he moved, which can make a man feel very unshaven.

He had had a lot of time to do some thinking since Thursday night, and as soon as he had got over feeling, in sequence, foolish, angry, and murderously vengeful, he had decided that the deaf man was responsible for what had happened to him. That was a good way to feel, he thought, because it took the blame away from two young punks (for Christ's sake, how could an experienced detective get smeared that way by two young punks?) and put it squarely onto a master criminal instead. Master criminals are very handy scapegoats, Carella reasoned, because they allow you to dismiss your own inadequacies. There was an old Jewish joke Meyer had once told him, about the mother who says to her son, "*Trombenik*, go get a job," and the son answers, "I can't, I'm a *trombenik*." The situation now was similar, he supposed, with the question being altered to read, "How can you let a master criminal do this to you?" and the logical answer being, "It's easy, he's a master criminal."

Whether or not the deaf man was a master criminal was perhaps a subject for debate. Carella would have to query his colleagues on the possibility of holding a seminar once he got back to the office. This, according to the interns who'd been examining his skull like phrenologists, should be by Thursday, it being their considered opinion that unconsciousness always meant concussion

and concussion always carried with it the possibility of
internal hemorrhage with at least a week's period of observation being *de rigueur* in such cases, go argue with
doctors.

Perhaps the deaf man wasn't a master criminal at all.
Perhaps he was simply smarter than any of the policemen he was dealing with, which encouraged some
pretty frightening conjecture. Given a superior intelligence at work, was it even *possible* for inferior intelli-
gences to second-guess whatever diabolical scheme was
afoot? Oh, come on now, Carella thought, diabolical indeed! Well, *yeah*, he thought, diabolical. It *is* diabolical
to demand five thousand dollars and then knock off the
parks commissioner, and it *is* diabolical to demand fifty
thousand dollars and then knock off the deputy mayor,
and it is staggering to imagine what the next demand
might be, or who the next victim would be. There most
certainly would be another demand which, if not met,
would doubtless lead to yet another victim. Or would it?
How can you second-guess a master criminal? You
can't, he's a master criminal.

No, Carella thought, he's only a human being, and
he's counting on several human certainties. He's hoping
to establish a pattern of warning and reprisal, he's
hoping we'll attempt to stop him each time, but only so
that we'll fail, forcing him to carry out his threat. Which
means that the two early extortion tries were only prepa-
ration for the big caper. And since he seems to be
climbing the municipal government ladder, and since he
multiplied his first demand by ten, I'm willing to bet his
next declared victim will be James Martin Vale, the

mayor himself, and that he'll ask for ten times what he asked for the last time: five hundred thousand dollars. That is a lot of strawberries.

Or am I only second-guessing a master criminal?

Am I *supposed* to be second-guessing him?

Is he really preparing the ground for a big killing, or is there quite another diabolical (there we go again) plan in his mind?

Teddy Carella walked into the room at that moment.

The only thing Carella had to second-guess was whether he would kiss her first or vice versa. Since his nose was in plaster, he decided to let her choose the target, which she did with practiced ease, causing him to consider some wildly diabolical schemes of his own, which if executed would have resulted in his never again being permitted inside Buena Vista Hospital.

Not even in a private room.

Patrolman Richard Genero was in the same hospital that Sunday morning, but his thoughts were less erotic than they were ambitious.

Despite a rather tight official security lid on the murders, an enterprising newspaperman had only this morning speculated on a possible connection between Genero's leg wound and the subsequent killing of Scanlon the night before. The police and the city officials had managed to keep all mention of the extortion calls and notes out of the newspapers thus far, but the reporter for the city's leading metropolitan daily wondered in print whether or not the detectives of "an uptown precinct bordering the park" hadn't in reality possessed foreknowledge of an attempt to be made on the deputy mayor's life, hadn't in fact set up an elaborate trap that very afternoon, "a trap in which a courageous patrolman was destined to suffer a bullet wound in the leg while attempting to capture the suspected killer." Wherever the reporter had dug up his information, he had neglected to mention that Genero had inflicted the wound upon himself, due to a fear of dogs and criminals, and due to a certain lack of familiarity with shooting at fleeing suspects.

Genero's father, who was a civil service employee himself, having worked for the Department of Sanitation for some twenty years now, was not aware that his son had accidentally shot himself in the leg. All he knew was that his son was a hero. As befitted a hero, he had brought a white carton of *cannoli* to the hospital, and now he and his wife and his son sat in the semi-private stillness of a fourth floor room and demolished the pastry while discussing Genero's almost certain promotion to Detective 3rd/Grade.

The idea of a promotion had not occurred to Genero before this, but as his father outlined the heroic action in the park the day before, Genero began to visualize himself as the man who had made the capture possible. Without him, without the warning shot he had fired into his own leg, the fleeing Alan Parry might never have stopped. The fact that Parry had turned out to be a wet fuse didn't matter at all to Genero. It was all well and good to realize a man wasn't dangerous *after* the fact, but where were all those detectives when Parry was running straight for Genero with a whole lunch pail full of

God-knew-what under his arm, where were they *then*, huh? And how could they have known *then*, while Genero was courageously drawing his pistol, that Parry would turn out to be only another innocent dupe, nossir, it had been impossible to tell.

"You were brave," Genero's father said, licking pot cheese from his lips. "It was *you* who tried to stop him."

"That's true," Genero said, because it *was* true.

"It was *you* who risked your life."

"That's right," Genero said, because it *was* right.

"They should promote you."

"They should," Genero said.

"I will call your boss," Genero's mother said.

"No, I don't think you should, Mama."

"Perchè no?"

"Perchè . . . Mama, please don't talk Italian, you know I don't understand Italian so well."

"Vergogna," his mother said, "an Italian doesn't understand his own tongue. I will call your boss."

"No, Mama, that isn't the way it's done."

"Then how *is* it done?" his father asked.

"Well, you've got to hint around."

"Hint? To who?"

"Well, to people."

"Which people?"

"Well, Carella's upstairs in this same hospital, maybe . . ."

"Ma chi è questa Carella?" his mother said.

"Mama, please."

"Who is this Carella?"

"A detective on the squad."

"Where you work, *sì*?"

"*Sì*. Please, Mama."

"He is your boss?"

"No, he just works up there."

"He was shot, too?"

"No, he was beat up."

"By the same man who shot you?"

"No, not by the same man who shot me," Genero said, which was also the truth.

"So what does he have to do with this?"

"Well, he's got influence."

"With the boss?"

"Well, no. You see, Captain Frick runs the entire precinct, he's actually the boss. But Lieutenant Byrnes is in charge of the detective squad, and Carella is a detective/2nd, and him and the lieutenant are like this, so maybe if I talk to Carella he'll see how I helped them grab that guy yesterday, and put in a good word for me."

"Let her call the boss," Genero's father said.

"No, it's better this way," Genero said.

"How much does a detective make?" Genero's mother asked.

"A fortune," Genero said.

Gadgets fascinated Detective-Lieutenant Sam Grossman, even when they were bombs. Or perhaps especially when they were bombs. There was no question in anyone's mind (how much question *could* there have been, considering the evidence of the demolished automobile and its five occupants?) that someone had put a bomb in the deputy mayor's car. Moreover, it was mandatory to assume that someone had set the bomb to go off at a specific time, rather than using the ignition wiring of the car as an immediate triggering device. This aspect of the puzzle pleased Grossman enormously because he considered ignition-trigger bombs to be rather crude devices capable of being wired by any gangland ape. *This* bomb was a time bomb. But it was a very special time bomb. It was a time bomb that had not been wired to the automobile clock.

How did Grossman know this?

Ah-ha, the police laboratory never sleeps, not even on Sunday. And besides, his technicians had found two clock faces in the rubble of the automobile.

One of the faces had been part of the Cadillac's dashboard clock. The other had come from a nationally advertised, popular-priced electric alarm clock. There was one other item of importance found in the rubble: a portion of the front panel of a DC-to-AC inverter, part of its brand name still showing where it was stamped into the metal.

These three parts lay on the counter in Grossman's laboratory like three key pieces to a jigsaw puzzle. All he had to do was fit them together and come up with a brilliant solution. He was feeling particularly brilliant this Sunday morning because his son had brought home a 92 on a high-school chemistry exam only two days ago; it always made Grossman feel brilliant when his son achieved anything. Well, let's see, he thought brilliantly. I've got three parts of a time bomb, or rather *two*

parts because I think I can safely eliminate the car's
clock except as a reference point. Whoever wired the
bomb undoubtedly refused to trust his own wrist watch
since a difference of a minute or two in timing might
have proved critical—in a minute, the deputy mayor
could have been out of the car already and on his way
into the synagogue. So he had set the electric clock with
the time showing on the dashboard clock. Why an *electric* clock? Simple. He did not want a clock that *ticked*.
Ticking might have attracted attention, especially if it
came from under the hood of a purring Cadillac. Okay,
so let's see what we've got. We've got an electric alarm
clock, and we've got a DC-to-AC inverter, which means
someone wanted to translate direct current to alternating
current. The battery in a Cadillac would have to be 12-
volts DC, and the electric clock would doubtless be
wired for alternating current. So perhaps we can reasonably assume that someone wanted to wire the clock to
the battery and needed an inverter to make this feasible.
Let's see.

He'd have had to run a positive lead to the battery
and a negative lead to any metal part of the automobile,
since the car itself would have served as a ground, right?
So now we've got a power source to the clock, and the
clock is running. Okay, right, the rest is simple, he'd
have had to use an electric blasting cap, sure, there'd
have been enough power to set one off, most commer-
cial electric detonators can be fired by passing a continuous current of 0.3 to 0.4 amperes through the bridge
wire. Okay, let's see, hold it now, let's look at it.

The battery provides our source of power . . .

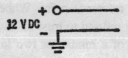

. . . to the inverter . . .

. . . and runs the electric clock . . .

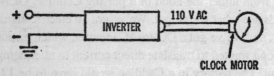

. . . . which is in turn set for a specific time, about eight, wasn't it? He'd have had to monkey around with the clock so that instead of the alarm ringing, a switch would close. That would complete the circuit, let's see, he'd have needed a lead running back to the battery, another lead running to the blasting cap, and a lead from the blasting cap to any metal part of the car. So that would look like . . .

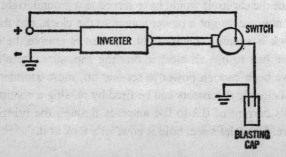

And that's it.

He could have assembled the entire package at home, taken it with him in a tool box, and wired it to the car in a very short time—making certain, of course, that all his wires were properly insulated, to guard against a stray current touching off a premature explosion. The only remaining question is how he managed to get access to the car, but happily that's not my problem.

Whistling brilliantly, Sam Grossman picked up the telephone and called Detective Meyer Meyer at the 87th.

The municipal garage was downtown on Dock Street, some seven blocks from City Hall. Meyer Meyer picked up Bert Kling at ten-thirty. The drive down along the River Dix took perhaps twenty minutes. They parked on a meter across the street from the big concrete and tile structure, and Meyer automatically threw the visor sign, even though this was Sunday and parking regulations were not in force.

The foreman of the garage was a man named Spencer Coyle.

He was reading Dick Tracy and seemed less impressed by the two detectives in his midst than by the fictional exploits of his favorite comic strip sleuth. It was only with a great effort of will that he managed to tear himself away from the newspaper at all. He did not rise from his chair, though. The chair was tilted back against the tiled wall of the garage. The tiles, a vomitous shade of yellow, decorated too many government buildings all over the city, and it was Meyer's guess that a hefty hunk of graft had influenced some purchasing agent back in the Thirties, either that or the poor bastard had been color-blind. Spencer Coyle leaned back in his chair against the tiles, his face long and gray and grizzled, his long legs stretched out in front of him, the comic section still dangling from his right hand, as though he were reluctant to let go of it completely even though he had stopped lip-reading it. He was wearing the greenish-brown coveralls of a Transportation Division employee, his peaked hat sitting on his head with all the rakish authority of a major in the Air Force. His attitude clearly told the detectives that he did not wish to be disturbed at *any* time, but especially on Sunday.

The detectives found him challenging.

"Mr. Coyle," Meyer said, "I've just had a telephone call from the police laboratory to the effect that the bomb . . ."

"What bomb?" Coyle asked, and spat on the floor, narrowly missing Meyer's polished shoe.

"The bomb that was put in the deputy mayor's Cadillac," Kling said, and hoped Coyle would spit again, but Coyle didn't.

"Oh, *that* bomb," Coyle said, as if bombs were put in every one of the city's Cadillacs regularly, making it difficult to keep track of all the bombs around. "What *about* that bomb?"

"The lab says it was a pretty complicated bomb, but that it couldn't have taken too long to wire to the car's battery, provided it had been assembled beforehand. Now, what we'd like to know . . ."

"Yeah, I'll bet it was complicated," Coyle said. He did not look into the faces of the detectives, but instead seemed to direct his blue-eyed gaze at a spot somewhere across the garage. Kling turned to see what he was staring at, but the only thing he noticed was another yellow tile wall.

"Would you have any idea who installed that bomb, Mr. Coyle?"

"*I* didn't," Coyle said flatly.

"Nobody suggested that you did," Meyer said.

"Just so we understand each other," Coyle said. "All I do is run this garage, make sure the cars are in working order, make sure they're ready to roll whenever somebody up there wants one, that's all I'm in charge of."

"How many cars do you have here?" Meyer asked.

"We got two dozen Caddys, twelve used on a regular basis, and the rest whenever we get visiting dignitaries. We also got fourteen buses and eight motorcycles. And there's also some vehicles that are kept here by the Department of Parks, but that's a courtesy because we got the space."

"Who services the cars?"

"Which ones?"

"The Caddys."

"Which one of the Caddys?" Coyle said, and spat again.

"Did you know, Mr. Coyle," Kling said, "that spitting on the sidewalk is a misdemeanor?"

"This ain't a sidewalk, this is my garage," Coyle said.

"This is city property," Kling said, "the equivalent of a sidewalk. In fact, since the ramp comes in directly from the street outside there, it could almost be considered an extension of the sidewalk."

"Sure," Coyle said. "You going to arrest me for it, or what?"

"You going to keep giving us a hard time?" Kling asked.

"Who's giving you a hard time?"

"We'd like to be home reading the funnies too," Kling said, "instead of out busting our asses on a bombing. Now how about it?"

"None of our mechanics put a bomb in that car," Coyle said flaty.

"How do you know?"

"Because I know all the men who work for me, and none of them put a bomb in that car, that's how I know."

"Who was here yesterday?" Meyer asked.

"I was."

"You were here alone?"

"No, the men were here too."

"Which men?"

"The mechanics."

"How many mechanics?"

"Two."

"Is that how many you usually have on duty?"

"We usually have six, but yesterday was Saturday, and we were working with a skeleton crew."

"Anybody else here?"

"Yeah, some of the chauffeurs were either picking up cars or bringing them back, they're in and out all the time. Also, there was supposed to be an outdoor fishing thing up in Grover Park, so we had a lot of bus drivers in. They were supposed to pick up these slum kids and take them to the park where they were going to fish through the ice on the lake. It got called off."

"Why?"

"Too cold."

"When were the bus drivers here?"

"They reported early in the morning, and they hung around till we got word it was called off."

"You see any of them fooling around near that Cad?"

"Nope. Listen, you're barking up the wrong tree. All those cars got checked out yesterday, and they were in A-number-One shape. That bomb must've been put in there *after* the car left the garage."

"No, that's impossible, Mr. Coyle."

"Well, it wasn't attached here."

"You're sure of that, are you?"

"I just told you the cars were inspected, didn't I?"

"Did you inspect them personally, Mr. Coyle?"

"No, I got other things to do besides inspecting two dozen Caddys and fourteen buses and eight motorcycles."

"Then who *did* inspect them, Mr. Coyle? One of your mechanics?"

"No, we had an inspector down from the Bureau of Motor Vehicles."

"And he said the cars were all right?"

"He went over them from top to bottom, every vehicle in the place. He gave us a clean bill of health."

"Did he look under the hoods?"

"Inside, outside, transmission, suspension, everything. He was here almost six hours."

"So he would have found a bomb if one was there, is that right?"

"That's right."

"Mr. Coyle, did he give you anything in writing to the effect that the cars were inspected and found in good condition?"

"Why?" Coyle asked. "You trying to get off the hook?"

"No, we're . . ."

"You trying to pass the buck to Motor Vehicles?"

"We're trying to find out how he could have missed the bomb that was undoubtedly under the hood of that car, that's what we're trying to do."

"It *wasn't*, that's your answer."

"Mr. Coyle, our lab reported . . ."

"I don't care what your lab reported or didn't report. I'm telling you all these cars were gone over with a fine-tooth comb yesterday, and there couldn't have been a bomb in the deputy mayor's car when it left this garage. Now that's *that*," Coyle said, and spat on the floor again, emphatically.

"Mr. Coyle," Kling said, "did you personally see the deputy mayor's car being inspected?"

"I personally saw it being inspected."

"You personally saw the hood being raised?"

"I did."

"And you'd be willing to swear that a thorough inspection was made of the area under the hood?"

"What do you mean?"

"Did you actually *see* the inspector checking the area under the hood?"

"Well, I didn't stand around looking over his shoulder, if that's what you mean."

"Where were you, actually, when the deputy mayor's car was being inspected?"

"I was right here."

"On this exact spot?"

"No, I was inside the office there. But I could see out into the garage. There's a glass panel in there."

"And you saw the inspector lifting the hood of the deputy mayor's car?"

"That's right."

"There are two dozen Caddys here. How'd you know that one was the deputy mayor's car?"

"By the license plate. It has DMA on it, and then the number. Same as Mayor Vale's car has MA on it for 'mayor,' and then the number. Same as the . . ."

"All right, it was clearly his car, and you definitely saw . . ."

"Look, that guy spent a good half-hour on each car, now don't tell *me* it wasn't a thorough inspection."

"Did he spend a half-hour on the deputy mayor's car?"

"Easily."

Meyer sighed. "I guess we'll have to talk to him personally," he said to Kling. He turned again to Coyle. "What was his name, Mr. Coyle?"

"Who?"

"The inspector. The man from Motor Vehicles."

"I don't know."

"He didn't give you his name?" Kling asked.

"He showed me his credentials, and he said he was here to inspect the cars, and that was that."

"What kind of credentials?"

"Oh, printed papers. You know."

"Mr. Coyle," Kling asked, "when was the last time a man from Motor Vehicles came to inspect?"

"This was the first time," Coyle said.

"They've never sent an inspector down before?"

"Never."

Slowly, wearily, Meyer said, "What did this man look like, Mr. Coyle?"

"He was a tall blond guy wearing a hearing aid," Coyle answered.

Fats Donner was a mountainous stool pigeon with a penchant for warm climates and the complexion of an Irish virgin. The complexion, in fact, overreached the boundaries of common definition to extend to every part of Donner's body; he was white all over, so sickly pale that sometimes Willis suspected him of being a junkie. Willis couldn't have cared less. On any given Sunday, a conscientious cop could collar seventy-nine junkies in a half-hour, seventy-eight of whom would be holding narcotics in some quantity. It was hard to come by a good informer, though, and Donner was one of the best around, *when* he was around. The difficulty with Donner was that he was likely to be found in Vegas or Miami Beach or Puerto Rico during the winter months, lying in the shade with his Buddha-like form protected against even a possible reflection of the sun's rays, quivering with delight as the sweat poured from his body.

Willis was surprised to find him in the city during the coldest March on record. He was not surprised to find him in a room that was suffocatingly hot, with three electric heaters adding their output to the two banging radiators. In the midst of this thermal onslaught, Donner sat in overcoat and gloves, wedged into a stuffed armchair. He was wearing two pairs of woolen socks, and his feet were propped up on the radiator. There was a girl in the room with him. She was perhaps fifteen years old, and she was wearing a flowered bra and bikini panties over which she had put on a silk wrapper. The wrapper was unbelted. The girl's near-naked body showed whenever she moved, but she seemed not to mind the presence of a strange man. She barely glanced at Willis when he came in, and then went about the room straightening up, never looking at either of the men as they whispered together near the window streaming wintry sunlight.

"Who's the girl?" Willis asked.

"My daughter," Donner said, and grinned.

He was not a nice man, Fats Donner, but he was a good stoolie, and criminal detection sometimes made strange bedfellows. It was Willis' guess that the girl was hooking for Donner, a respectable stoolie sometimes being in need of additional income which he can realize, for example, by picking up a little girl straight from Ohio and teaching her what it's all about and then putting her on the street, there are more things in heaven and earth, Horatio. Willis was not interested in Donner's possible drug habit, nor was Willis interested in hanging a prostitution rap on the girl, nor in busting Donner as a "male person living on the proceeds of prostitution," Section 1148 of the Penal Law. Willis was interested in taking off his coat and hat and finding out whether or not Donner could give him a line on a man named Dom.

"Dom who?" Donner asked.

"That's all we've got."

"How many Doms you suppose are in this city?" Donner asked. He turned to the girl, who was puttering around rearranging food in the refrigerator, and said, "Mercy, how many Doms you suppose are in this city?"

"I don't know," Mercy replied without looking at him.

"How many Doms you know personally?" Donner asked her.

"I don't know any Doms," the girl said. She had a tiny voice, tinged with an unmistakable Southern accent. Scratch Ohio, Willis thought, substitute Arkansas or Tennessee.

"She don't know any Doms," Donner said, and chuckled.

"How about you, Fats? You know any?"

"That's all you're giving me?" Donner asked. "Man, you're really generous."

"He lost a lot of money on the championship fight two weeks ago."

"Everybody I *know* lost a lot of money on the championship fight two weeks ago."

"He's broke right now. He's trying to promote some scratch," Willis said.

"Dom, huh?"

"Yeah."

"From this part of the city?"

"A friend of his lives in Riverhead," Willis said.

"What's the friend's name?"

"La Bresca. Tony La Bresca."

"What about *him*?"

"No record."

"You think this Dom done time?"

"I've got no idea. He seems to have tipped to a caper that's coming off."

"Is that what you're interested in? The caper?"

"Yes. According to him, the buzz is all over town."

"There's always some buzz or other that's all over town," Donner said. "What the hell are you doing there, Mercy?"

"Just fixing things," Mercy said.

"Get the hell away from there, you make me nervous."

"I was just fixing the things in the fridge," Mercy said.

"I hate that Southern accent," Donner said. "Don't you hate Southern accents?" he asked Willis.

"I don't mind them," Willis said.

"Can't even understand her half the time. Sounds as if she's got shit in her mouth."

The girl closed the refrigerator door and went to the closet. She opened the door and began moving around empty hangers.

"*Now* what're you doing?" Donner asked.

"Just straightening things," she said.

"You want me to kick you out in the street bare-assed?" Donner asked.

"No," she said softly.

"Then cut it out."

"All right."

"Anyway, it's time you got dressed."

"All right."

"Go on, go get dressed. What time is it?" he asked Willis.

"Almost noon," Willis said.

"Sure, go get dressed," Donner said.

"All right," the girl said, and went into the other room.

"Damn little bitch," Donner said, "hardly worth keeping around."

"I thought she was your daughter," Willis said.

"Oh, is that what you thought?" Donner asked, and again he grinned.

Willis restrained a sudden impulse. He sighed and said, "So what do you think?"

"I don't think nothing yet, man. Zero so far."

"Well, you want some time on it?"

"How much of a sweat are you in?"

"We need whatever we can get as soon as we can get it."

"What's the caper sound like?"

"Maybe extortion."

"Dom, huh?"

"Dom," Willis repeated.

"That'd be for Dominick, right?"

"Yes."

"Well, let me listen around, who knows?"

The girl came out of the other room. She was wearing a miniskirt and white mesh stockings, a low-cut purple blouse. There was smear of bright red lipstick on her mouth, green eyeshadow on her eyelids.

"You going down now?" Donner asked.

"Yes," she answered.

"Put on your coat."

"All right," she said.

"And take your bag."

"I will."

"Don't come back empty, baby," Donner said.

"I won't," she said, and moved toward the door.

"I'm going too," Willis said.

"I'll give you a buzz."

"Okay, but try to move fast, will you?" Willis said.

"It's I hate to go out when it's so fucking cold," Donner answered.

The girl was on the hallway steps, below Willis, walking down without any sense of haste, buttoning her coat, slinging her bag over her shoulder. Willis caught up with her and said, "Where are you from, Mercy?"

"Ask Fats," she answered.

"I'm asking *you*."

"You fuzz?"

"That's right."

"Georgia," she said.

"When'd you get up here?"

"Two months ago."

"How old are you?"

"Sixteen."

"What the hell are you doing with a man like Fats Donner?" Willis asked.

"I don't know," she said. She would not look into his face. She kept her head bent as they went down the steps to the street. As Willis opened the door leading outside, a blast of frigid air rushed into the hallway.

"Why don't you get out?" he said.

The girl looked up at him.

"Where would I go?" she asked, and then left him on the stoop, walking up the street with a practiced swing, the bag dangling from her shoulder, her high heels clicking along the pavement.

At two o'clock that afternoon, the seventeen-year-old girl who had been in the convertible that crashed the river barrier died without gaining consciousness.

The Buena Vista Hospital record read simply: Death secondary to head injury.

THE SQUADROOM PHONE BEGAN JANGLING EARLY
Monday morning.

The first call was from a reporter on the city's austere
morning daily. He asked to speak to whoever was in
charge of the squad and, when told that Lieutenant
Byrnes was not in at the moment, asked to speak to whoever was in command.

"This is Detective 2nd/Grade Meyer Meyer," he was
told. "I suppose I'm in command at the moment."

"Detective Meyer," the reporter said, "this is Carlyle
Butterford, I wanted to check out a possible story."

At first, Meyer thought the call was a put-on, nobody
had a name like Carlyle Butterford. Then he remembered that *everybody* on this particular morning newspaper had names like Preston Fingerlaver, or Clyde

Masterfield, or Aylmer Coopermere. "Yes, Mr. Butterford," he said, "What can I do for you?"

"We received a telephone call early this morning . . ."

"From whom, sir?"

"An anonymous caller," Butterford said.

"Yes?"

"Yes, and he suggested that we contact the 87th Precinct regarding certain extortion calls and notes that were received before the deaths of Parks Commissioner Cowper and Deputy Mayor Scanlon."

There was a long silence on the line.

"Detective Meyer, is there any truth to this allegation?"

"I suggest that you call the Public Relations Officer of the Police Department," Meyer said, "his name is Detective Glenn, and he's downtown at Headquarters. The number there is Center 6-0800."

"Would he have any knowledge of these alleged extortion calls and notes?" Butterford asked.

"I guess you'd have to ask him," Meyer said.

"Do *you* have any knowledge of these alleged . . . ?"

"As I told you," Meyer said, "the lieutenant is out at the moment, and he's the one who generally supplies information to the press."

"But would *you*, personally, have any information . . . ?"

"I have information on a great many things," Meyer said. "Homicides, muggings, burglaries, robberies, rapes, extortion attempts, all sorts of things. But, as I'm sure you know, detectives are public servants and it has been the department's policy to discourage us from seeking personal aggrandizement. If you wish to talk to the lieutenant, I suggest you call back at around ten o'clock. He should be in by then."

"Come on," Butterford said, "give me a break."

"I'm sorry, pal, I can't help you."

"I'm a working stiff, just like you."

"So's the lieutenant," Meyer said, and hung up.

The second call came at nine-thirty. Sergeant Murchison, at the switchboard, took the call and immediately put it through to Meyer.

"This is Cliff Savage," the voice said. "Remember me?"

"Only too well," Meyer said. "What do you want, Savage?"

"Carella around?"

"Nope."

"Where is he?"

"Out," Meyer said.

"I wanted to talk to him."

"He doesn't want to talk to you," Meyer said. "You almost got his wife killed once with your goddamn yellow journalism. You want my advice, keep out of his sight."

"I guess I'll have to talk to you, then," Savage said.

"I'm not too fond of you myself, if you want the truth."

"Well, thank you," Savage said, "but that's not the truth I'm after."

"What *are* you after?"

"I got a phone call this morning from a man who refused to identify himself. He gave me a very interesting piece of information." Savage paused. "Know anything about it?"

Meyer's heart was pounding, but he very calmly said, "I'm not a mind reader, Savage."

"I thought you might know something about it."

"Savage, I've given you the courtesy of five minutes of valuable time already. Now if you've got something to say . . ."

"Okay, okay. The man I spoke to said the 87th Precinct had received several threatening telephone calls preceding the death of Parks Commissioner Cowper, and three extortion notes preceding the death of Deputy Mayor Scanlon. Know anything about it?"

"Telephone company'd probably be able to help you on any phone calls you want to check, and I guess the Documents Section of the Public Library . . ."

"Come on, Meyer, don't stall me."

"We're not permitted to give information to reporters," Meyer said. "You know that."

"How much do you want, Meyer?"

"How much can you afford?" Meyer asked.

"How does a hundred bucks sound?"

"Not so good."

"How about two hundred?"

"I get more than that just for protecting our friendly neighborhood pusher."

"Three hundred is my top offer," Savage said.

"Would you mind repeating the offer for the benefit of the tape recorder?" Meyer said. "I want to have evidence when I charge you with attempting to bribe a police officer."

"I was merely offering you a loan," Savage said.

"Neither a borrower nor a lender be," Meyer said, and hung up.

This was not good. This was, in fact, bad. He was about to dial the lieutenant's home number, hoping to catch him before he left for the office, when the telephone on his desk rang again.

"87th Squad," he said, "Detective Meyer."

The caller was from one of the two afternoon papers. He repeated essentially what Meyer had already heard from his two previous callers, and then asked if Meyer knew anything about it. Meyer, loath to lie lest the story eventually broke and tangentially mentioned that there had been a police credibility gap, suggested that the man try the lieutenant later on in the day. When he hung up, he looked at the clock and decided to wait for the next call before trying to contact the lieutenant. Fortunately, there were now only four daily newspapers in the city, the leaders of the various newspaper guilds and unions having decided that the best way to ensure higher wages and lifetime employment was to make demands that would kill off the newspapers one by one, leaving behind only scattered goose feathers and broken golden egg shells. Meyer did not have to wait long. The representative of the fourth newspaper called within five minutes. He had a bright chirpy voice and an ingratiating style. He got nothing from Meyer, and he finally hung up in cheerful rage.

It was now five minutes to ten, too late to catch Byrnes at home.

While he waited for the lieutenant to arrive, Meyer

doodled a picture of a man in a fedora shooting a Colt .45
automatic. The man looked very much like Meyer, except that he possessed a full head of hair. Meyer had
once possessed a full head of hair. He tried to remember
when. It was probably when he was ten years old. He
was smiling painfully over his own joke when Byrnes
came into the squadroom. The lieutenant looked dys-
peptic this morning. Meyer surmised that he missed the
painters. Everyone on the squad missed the painters.
They had added humanity to the joint, and richness, a
spirit of gregarious joy, a certain *je ne sais quoi*.

"We got trouble," Meyer said, but before he could re-
late the trouble to the lieutenant, the phone rang again.
Meyer lifted the receiver, identified himself, and then
looked at Byrnes.

"It's the Chief of Detectives," he said, and Byrnes
sighed and went to his office to take the call privately.

Thirty-three telephone calls were exchanged that
morning as police and city government officials kept the
wires hot between their own offices and Lieutenant
Byrnes', trying to decide what to do about this latest re-
volting development. The one thing they did not need on
this case was publicity that would make them all appear
foolish. And yet, if there really *had* been a leak about the
extortion attempts, it seemed likely that the full story
might come to light at any moment, in which case it
might be best to level with the papers *before* they broke
the news. At the same time, the anonymous caller might
only have been speculating, without any real evidence to
back up his claim of extortion, in which case a prema-

ture release to the newspapers would only serve to breach a danger that was not truly threatening. What to do, oh, what to do?

The telephones rang, and the possibilities multiplied. Heads swam and tempers flared. The mayor, James Martin Vale himself, postponed a walking trip from City Hall to Grover Park and personally called Lieutenant Byrnes to ask his opinion on "the peril of the situation." Lieutenant Byrnes passed the buck to the Chief of Detectives who in turn passed it back to Captain Frick of the 87th, who referred JMV's secretary to the police commissioner, who for reasons unknown said he must first consult with the traffic commissioner, who in turn referred the police commissioner to the Bridge Authority who somehow got on to the city comptroller, who in turn called JMV himself to ask what this was all about.

At the end of two hours of dodging and wrangling, it was decided to take the bull by the horns and release transcripts of the telephone conversations, as well as photocopies of the three notes, to all four city newspapers. The city's liberal blue-headline newspaper (which was that week running an exposé on the growth of the numbers racket as evidenced by the prevalence of nickel and dime betters in kindergarten classes) was the first paper to break the story, running photos of the three notes side by side on its front page. The city's other afternoon newspaper, recently renamed the *Pierce-Arrow-Universal-International-Bugle-Chronicle-Clarion* or something, was next to feature the notes on its front page, together with transcripts of the calls in 24-point Cheltenham Bold.

That night, the early editions of the two morning newspapers carried the story as well. This meant that a combined total of four million readers now knew all about the extortion threats.

The next move was anybody's.

Anthony La Bresca and his pool hall buddy, Peter Vincent Calucci (alias Calooch, Cooch, or Kook) met in a burlesque house on a side street off The Stem at seven o'clock that Monday night.

La Bresca had been tailed from his place of employment, a demolition site in the city's downtown financial district, by three detectives using the ABC method of surveillance. Mindful of the earlier unsuccessful attempts to keep track of him, nobody was taking chances anymore—the ABC method was surefire and foolproof.

Detective Bob O'Brien was "A," following La Bresca while Detective Andy Parker, who was "B," walked behind O'Brien and kept him constantly in view. Detective Carl Kapek was "C," and he moved parallel with La Bresca, on the opposite side of the street. This meant that if La Bresca suddenly went into a coffee shop or ducked around the corner, Kapek could instantly swap places with O'Brien, taking the lead "A" position while O'Brien caught up, crossed the street, and maneuvered into the "C" position. It also meant that the men could use camouflaging tactics at their own discretion, changing positions so that the combination became BCA or CBA or CAB or whatever they chose, a scheme that guaranteed La Bresca would not recognize any one man following him over an extended period of time.

Wherever he went, La Bresca was effectively contained. Even in parts of the city where the crowds were unusually thick, there was no danger of losing him. Kapek would merely cross over onto La Bresca's side of the street and begin walking some fifteen feet *ahead* of him, so that the pattern read C, La Bresca, A, and B. In police jargon, they were "sticking like a dirty shirt," and they did their job well and unobtrusively, despite the cold weather and despite the fact that La Bresca seemed to be a serendipitous type who led them on a jolly excursion halfway across the city, apparently trying to kill time before his seven-o'clock meeting with Calucci.

The two men took seats in the tenth row of the theater. The show was in progress, two baggy-pants comics relating a traffic accident one of them had had with a car driven by a voluptuous blonde.

"You mean she crashed right into your tail pipe?" one of the comics asked.

"Hit me with her headlights," the second one said.

"Hit your tail pipe with her headlights?" the first one asked.

"Almost broke it off for me," the second one said.

Kapek, taking a seat across the aisle from Calucci and La Bresca, was suddenly reminded of the squadroom painters and realized how sorely he missed their presence. O'Brien had moved into the row behind the pair, and was sitting directly back of them now. Andy Parker was in the same row, two seats to the left of Calucci.

"Any trouble getting here?" Calucci whispered.

"No," La Bresca whispered back.

"What's with Dom?"

"He wants in."

"I thought he just wanted a couple of bills."

"That was last week."

"What's he want now?"

"A three-way split."

"Tell him to go screw," Calucci said.

"No. He's hip to the whole thing."

"How'd he find out?"

"I don't know. But he's hip, that's for sure."

There was a blast from the trumpet section of the four-piece band in the pit. The overhead leikos came up purple, and a brilliant follow spot hit the curtain stage left. The reed section followed the heraldic trumpet with a saxophone obbligato designed to evoke memory or desire or both. A gloved hand snaked its way around the curtain. "And now," a voice said over the loudspeaker system while one-half of the rhythm section started a snare drum roll, "and *now*, for the first time in America, direct from Brest, which is where the little lady comes from . . . exhibiting her titillating terpsichoreal skills for your pleasure, we are happy to present Miss . . . Freida Panzer!"

A leg appeared from behind the curtain.

It floated disembodied on the air. A black high-heeled pump pointed, wiggled, a calf muscle tightened, the knee bent, and then the toe pointed again. There was more of the leg visible now, the black nylon stocking shimmered in the glow of the lights, ribbed at the top where a vulnerable white thigh lay exposed, black garter biting into the flesh, fetishists all over the theater thrilled to the sight, not to mention a few detectives who weren't fetishists at all. Freida Panzer undulated onto the stage bathed in the glow of the overhead purple leikos, wearing a long purple gown slit up each leg to the waist, the black stockings and taut black garters revealed each time she took another long-legged step across the stage.

"Look at them legs," Calucci whispered.

"Yeah," La Bresca said.

O'Brien, sitting behind them, looked at the legs. They were extraordinary legs.

"I hate to cut anybody else in on this," Calucci whispered.

"Me, neither," La Bresca said, "but what else can we do? He'll run screaming to the cops if we don't play ball."

"Is that what he said?"

"Not in so many words. He just hinted."

"Yeah, the son of a bitch."

"So what do you think?" La Bresca asked.

"Man, there's big money involved here," Calucci said.

"You think I don't know?"

"Why cut him in after we done all the planning?"

"What else can we do?"

"We can wash him," Calucci whispered.

The girl was taking off her clothes.

The four-piece ensemble in the orchestra pit rose to heights of musical expression, a heavy bass drum beat accentuating each solid bump as purple clothing fell like aster petals, a triple-tongued trumpet winding up with each pelvic grind, a saxophone wail climbing the girl's flanks in accompaniment with her sliding hands, a steady piano beat banging out the rhythm of each long-legged stride, each tassel-twirling, fixed-grin, sexy-eyed, contrived, and calculated erotic move. "She's got some tits," Calucci whispered, and La Bresca whispered back, "Yeah."

The men fell silent.

The music rose in earsplitting crescendo. The bass drum beat was more insistent now, the trumpet shrieked higher and higher, a C above high C reached for and missed, the saxophone trilled impatiently, the piano pounded in the upper register, a tinny insistent honky-tonk rhythm, cymbals clashed, the trumpet reached for the screech note again, and again missed. The lights were swirling now, the stage was inundated in color and sound. There was the stink of perspiration and lust in the theater as the girl ground out her coded message in a cipher broken long ago on too many similar stages, pounded out her promises of ecstasy and sin. Come and get it, baby, Come and get it, Come and come and come and come.

The stage went black.

In the darkness, Calucci whispered, "What do you think?"

One of the baggy pants comics came on again to do a bit in a doctor's office accompanied by a pert little blonde with enormous breasts who explained that she thought she was stagnant because she hadn't fenestrated in two months.

"I hate the idea of knocking somebody off," La Bresca whispered.

"If it's necessary, it's necessary."

"Still."

"There's lots of money involved here, don't forget it."

"Yeah, but at the same time, there's enough to split three ways, ain't there ?" La Bresca said.

"Why should we split it three ways when we can split it down the middle?"

"Because Dom'll spill the whole works if we don't cut him in. Look, what's the sense going over this a hundred times? We *got* to cut him in."

"I want to think about it."

"You ain't got that much time to think about it. We're set for the fifteenth. Dom wants to know right away."

"Okay, so tell him he's in. Then we'll decide whether he's in or out. And I mean *really* out, the little son of a bitch."

"And now, ladies and gentlemen," the loudspeaker voice said, "it gives us great pleasure to present the rage of San Francisco, a young lady who thrilled the residents of that city by the Golden Gate, a young lady whose exotic dancing caused the pious officials of Hong Kong to see Red . . . it is with bursting pride that we turn our stage over to Miss . . . *Anna . . . May . . . Zong!*"

The house lights dimmed. The band struck up a sinuous version of "Limehouse Blues." A swish cymbal echoed on the air, and a sloe-eyed girl wearing mandarin garb came into the follow spot with mincing steps, hands together in an attitude of prayer, head bent.

"I dig these Chinks," Calucci said.

"You guys want to stop talking?" a bald-headed man in the row ahead said. "I can't see the girls with all that gabbing behind me."

"Fuck off, Baldy," La Bresca said.

But both men fell silent. O'Brien leaned forward in his seat. Parker bent sideways over the armrest. There was nothing further to hear. Kapek, across the aisle, could not have heard anything anyway, so he merely watched the Chinese girl as she took off her clothes.

At the end of the act, La Bresca and Calucci rose quietly from their seats and went out of the theater. They split up outside. Parker followed Calucci to his house, and Kapek followed La Bresca to his. O'Brien went back to the squadroom to type up a report.

The detectives did not get together again until eleven o'clock that night, by which time La Bresca and Calucci were both hopefully asleep. They met in a diner some five blocks from the squadroom. Over coffee and crullers, they all agreed that the only thing they'd learned from their eavesdropping was the date of the job La Bresca and Calucci were planning: March the fifteenth. They also agreed that Freida Panzer had much larger breasts than Anna May Zong.

In the living room of a luxurious apartment on Harborside Oval, overlooking the river, a good three miles from where Detectives O'Brien, Parker, and Kapek were speculating on the comparative dimensions of the two strippers, the deaf man sat on a sofa facing sliding glass doors, and happily sipped at a glass of scotch and soda. The drapes were open, and the view of warm and glowing lights strung on the bridge's cables, the distant muted reds and ambers blinking on the distant shore, gave the night a deceptively springtime appearance; the thermometer on the terrace outside read ten degrees above zero.

Two bottles of expensive scotch, one already dead, were on the coffee table before the sofa upholstered in rich black leather. On the wall opposite the sofa, there hung an original Rouault, only a gouache to be sure, but nonetheless quite valuable. A grand piano turned its wide curve into the room, and a petite brunette, wearing a miniskirt and a white crocheted blouse, sat at the piano playing "Heart and Soul" over and over again.

The girl was perhaps twenty-three years old, with a nose that had been recently bobbed, large brown eyes, long black hair that fell to a point halfway between her waist and her shoulder blades. She was wearing false eyelashes. They fluttered whenever she hit a sour note, which was often. The deaf man seemed not to mind the discord that rose from the piano. Perhaps he really *was* deaf, or perhaps he had consumed enough scotch to have dimmed his perception. The two other men in the room didn't seem to mind the cacophony either. One of them even tried singing along with the girl's treacherous rendition—until she hit another sour note and began again from the top.

"I can't seem to get it," she said, pouting.

"You'll get it, honey," the deaf man said. "Just keep at it."

One of the men was short and slender, with the dust-colored complexion of an Indian. He wore narrow black tapered trousers and a white shirt over which was an open black vest. He was sitting at a drop-leaf desk, typing. The other man was tall and burly, with blue eyes, red hair, and a red mustache. There were freckles spattered over his cheeks and his forehead, and his voice, as he began singing along with the girl again, was deep and resonant. He was wearing tight jeans and a blue turtleneck sweater.

As the girl continued to play "Heart and Soul," a feeling of lassitude spread through the deaf man. Sitting on the couch, watching the second phase of his scheme as it became a reality, he mused again on the beauty of the plan, and then glanced at the girl, and then smiled when she hit the same sour note (an E flat where it should have been a natural E) and then looked again to where Ahmad was typing.

"The beauty of this phase," he said aloud, "is that none of them will believe us."

"They will believe," Ahmad offered, and smiled thinly.

"Yes, but not at this phase."

"No, only later," Ahmad said, and sipped at his scotch, and glanced at the girl's thighs, and went back to his typing.

"How much is this mailing going to cost us?" the other man asked.

"Well, Buck," the deaf man said, "we're sending out a hundred pieces of first-class mail at five cents postage per envelope, so that comes to a grand total of five dollars—if my arithmetic is correct."

"Your arithmetic is *always* correct," Ahmad said, and smiled.

"*This* is the damn part I can't get," the girl said, and

struck the same note over and over again, as though trying to pound it into her memory.

"Keep at it, Rochelle," the deaf man said. "You'll get it."

Buck lifted his glass, discovered it was empty, and went to the coffee table to refill it, moving with the economy of an athlete, back ramrod stiff, hands dangling loosely at his sides, as though he were going back for the huddle after having executed a successful line plunge.

"Here, let me help you," the deaf man said.

"Not too heavy," Buck said.

The deaf man poured a liberal shot into Buck's extended glass. "Drink," he said. "You deserve it."

"Well, I don't want to get crocked."

"Why not? You're among friends," the deaf man said, and smiled.

He was feeling particularly appreciative of Buck's talent tonight, because without it this phase of the scheme would never have become a reality. Oh yes, a primitive bomb *could* have been assembled and hastily wired to the ignition switch, but such sloppiness, such dependency on chance, had never appealed to the deaf man. The seriousness with which Buck had approached the problem had been truly heart-warming. His development of a compact package (the inverter had weighed a mere twenty-two pounds and measured only ten by ten by five) that could be easily transported and wired in a relatively short period of time, his specific demand for an inverter with a regulated sine-wave output (costing a bit more, yes, $64.95, but a negligible output in terms of the hoped-for financial realization), his insistence on a briefing session to explain the proper handling of the dynamite and the electric blasting cap, all were admirable, admirable. He was a good man, Buck, a demolition expert who had worked on countless legitimate blasting jobs, a background essential to the deaf man's plan; in this state, you were not allowed to buy explosives without a permit and insurance, both of which Buck possessed. The deaf man was very pleased indeed to have him in his employ.

Ahmad, too, was indispensable. He had been working as a draftsman at Metropolitan Power & Light, earning $150 a week in the Bureau of Maps and Records, when the deaf man first contacted him. He had readily appreciated the huge rewards to be reaped from the scheme, and had enthusiastically supplied all of the information so necessary to its final phase. In addition, he was a meticulous little man who had insisted that all of these letters be typed on high-quality bond paper, with each of the hundred men receiving an original rather than a carbon or a photocopy, a touch designed to allay any suspicion that the letter was a practical joke. The deaf man knew that the difference between success and failure very often depended on such small details, and he smiled at Ahmad in appreciation now, and sipped a little more of his scotch, and said, "How many have you typed so far?"

"Fifty-two."

"We'll be toiling long into the night, I'm afraid."

"When are we going to mail these?"

"I had hoped by Wednesday."

"I will finish them long before then," Ahmad promised.

"Will you really be working here all night?" Rochelle asked, pouting again.

"You can go to bed if you like, dear," the deaf man said.

"What good's bed without you?" Rochelle said, and Buck and Ahmad exchanged glances.

"Go on, I'll join you later."

"I'm not sleepy."

"Then have a drink, and play us another song."

"I don't know any other songs."

"Read a book then," the deaf man suggested.

Rochelle looked at him blankly.

"Or go into the den and watch some television."

"There's nothing on but old movies."

"Some of those old films are very instructive," the deaf man said.

"Some of them are very crappy, too," Rochelle replied.

The deaf man smiled. "Do you feel like licking a hundred envelopes?" he asked.

"No, I don't feel like licking envelopes," she answered.

"I didn't think so," the deaf man said.

"So what should I do?" Rochelle asked.

"Go get into your nightgown, darling," the deaf man said.

"Mmm?" she said, and looked at him archly.

"Mmm," he replied.

"Okay," she said, and rose from the piano bench. "Well, good night, fellas," she said.

"Good night," Buck said.

"Good night, miss," Ahmad said.

Rochelle looked at the deaf man again, and then went into the other room.

"Empty-headed little bitch," he said.

"I think she's dangerous to have around," Buck said.

"On the contrary," the deaf man said, "she soothes the nerves and eases the daily pressures. Besides, she thinks we're respectable businessmen promoting some sort of hare-brained scheme. She hasn't the vaguest notion of what we're up to."

"Sometimes *I* don't have the vaguest notion either," Buck said, and pulled a face.

"It's really very simple," the deaf man said. "We're making a direct-mail appeal, a tried-and-true method of solicitation pioneered by businessmen all over this bountiful nation. *Our* mailing, of course, is a limited one. We're only sending out a hundred letters. But it's my hope that we'll get a highly favorable response."

"And what if we don't?"

"Well, Buck, let's assume the worst. Let's assume we get a one-percent return, which is the generally expected return on a direct-mail piece. Our entire outlay thus far has been $86.95 for a lever-action carbine; $3.75 for a box of cartridges; $64.95 for your inverter; $7.00 for the electric clock; $9.60 for a dozen sticks of dynamite at eighty cents a stick; sixty cents for the blasting cap; $10.00 for the stationery; and $5.00 for the postage. If my addition is correct . . ." (He paused here to smile at Ahmad.) ". . . that comes to $187.85. Our future expenses—for the volt-ohm meter, the pressure-sensitive letters, the uniform, and so on—should also be negligible. Now, if we get only a one-percent return on our mailing, it only *one* person out of the hundred comes through, we'll *still* be reaping a large profit on our initial investment."

"Five thousand dollars seems like pretty small change for two murders," Buck said.

"*Three* murders," the deaf man corrected.

"Even better," Buck said, and pulled a face.

"I assure you I'm expecting much more than a one-percent return. On Friday night, we execute—if you'll pardon the pun—the final phase of our plan. By Saturday morning, there'll be no disbelievers."

"How many of them do you think'll come through?"

"Most of them. If not all of them."

"And what about the fuzz?"

"What about them? They *still* don't know who we are, and they'll never find out."

"I hope you're right."

"I *know* I'm right."

"I worry about fuzz," Buck said. "I can't help it. I've been conditioned to worry about them."

"There's nothing to worry about. Don't you *realize* why they're called fuzz?"

"No. Why?"

"Because they're fuzzy and fussy and antiquated and incompetent. Their investigatory technique is established and routine, designed for effectiveness in an age that no longer exists. The police in this city are like wind-up toys with keys sticking out of their backs, capable of performing only in terms of their own limited design, tiny mechanical men clattering along the sidewalk stiff-legged, scurrying about in aimless circles. But put an obstacle in their path, a brick wall or an orange crate, and they unwind helplessly in the same spot, arms and legs thrashing but taking them nowhere." The deaf man grinned. "I, my friend, am the brick wall."

"Or the orange crate," Buck said.

"No," Ahmad said intensely. "He is the brick wall."

10

THE FIRST BREAK IN THE CASE CAME AT TEN O'CLOCK THE next morning, when Fats Donner called the squadroom.

Until that time, there were still perhaps two thousand imponderables to whatever La Bresca and Calucci were planning. But aside from such minor considerations as *where* the job would take place, or at exactly what *time* on March fifteenth, there were several unknown identities to contend with as well, such as Dom (who so far had no last name) and the long-haired blond girl who had given La Bresca a lift last Friday night. It was the police supposition that if either of these two people could be located, the nature of the impending job might be wrung from one or the other of them. Whether or not the job was in any way connected with the recent murders would then become a matter for further speculation, as would the possibility that La Bresca was in some way involved with the deaf man. There were a lot of questions to be asked if only they could find somebody to ask them to.

Donner was put through immediately.

"I think I got your Dom," he said to Willis.

"Good," Willis said. "What's his last name?"

"Di Fillippi. Dominick Di Fillippi. Lives in Riverhead near the old coliseum, you know the neighborhood?"

"Yeah. What've you got on him?"

"He's with The Coaxial Cable."

"Yeah?" Willis said.

"Yeah."

"Well, what's that?" Willis said.

"What's *what*?"

"What's it supposed to *mean*?"

"What's *what* supposed to mean?"

"What you just said. Is it some kind of code or something?"

"Is what some kind of code?" Donner asked.

"The Coaxial Cable."

"No, it's a group."

"A group of *what*?"

"A group. Musicians," Donner said.

"A band, you mean?"

"That's right, only today they call them groups."

"Well, what's the coaxial cable got to do with it?"

"That's the name of the group. The Coaxial Cable."

"You're putting me on," Willis said.

"No, that's the name, I mean it."

"What does Di Fillippi play?"

"Rhythm guitar."

"Where do I find him?"

"His address is 365 North Anderson."

"That's in Riverhead?"

"Yeah."

"How do you know he's our man?"

"Well, it seems he's a big bullshit artist, you know?" Donner said. "He's been going around the past few weeks saying he dropped a huge bundle on the championship fight, made it sound like two, three G's. It turns out all he lost was fifty bucks, that's some big bundle, huh?"

"Yeah, go ahead."

"But he's also been saying recently that he knows about a big caper coming off."

"Who'd he say this to?"

"Well, one of the guys in the group is a big hophead from back even before it got stylish. That's how I got my lead onto Di Fillippi. And the guy said they were busting some joints together maybe three, four days ago, and Di Fillippi came on about this big caper he knew about."

"Did he say what the caper was?"

"No."

"And they were smoking pot?"

"Yeah, busting a few joints, you know, social."

"Maybe Di Fillippi was out of his skull."

"He probably was. What's that got to do with it?"

"He might have dreamt up the whole thing."

"I don't think so."

"Did he mention La Bresca at all?"

"Nope."

"Did he say when the job would be coming off?"

"Nope."

"Well, it's not much, Fats."

"It's worth half a century, don't you think?"

"It's worth ten bucks," Willis said.

"Hey, come on, man, I had to do some real hustling to get this for you."

"Which reminds me," Willis said.

"Huh?"

"Get rid of your playmate."

"Huh?"

"The girl. Next time I see you, I want her out of there."

"Why?"

"Because I thought it over, and I don't like the idea."

"I kicked her out twice already," Donner said. "She always comes back."

"Then maybe you ought to use this ten bucks to buy her a ticket back to Georgia."

"Sure. Maybe I ought to contribute another ten besides to the Salvation Army," Donner said.

"Just get her out of there," Willis said.

"When'd you get so righteous?" Donner asked.

"Just this minute."

"I thought you were a businessman."

"I am. Here's my deal. Let the girl go, and I forget whatever else I know about you, and whatever I might learn in the future."

"Nobody learns nothing about me," Donner said. "I'm The Shadow."

"No," Willis said. "Only Lamont Cranston is The Shadow."

"You serious about this?"

"I want the girl out of there. If she's still around next time I see you, I throw the book."

"And lose a valuable man."

"Maybe," Willis said. "In which case, we'll have to manage without you somehow."

"Sometimes I wonder why I bother helping you guys at all," Donner said.

"I'll *tell* you why sometime, if you have a minute," Willis said.

"Never mind."

"Will you get the girl out of there?"

"Yeah, yeah. You're going to send me fifty, right?"

"I said ten."

"Make it twenty."

"For the birdseed you just gave me?"

"It's a lead, ain't it?"

"That's all it is."

"So? A lead is worth at least twenty-five."

"I'll send you fifteen," Willis said, and hung up.

The phone rang again almost the instant he replaced it on the cradle. He lifted the receiver and said, "87th, Willis speaking."

"Hal, this is Artie over at the school."

"Yep."

"I've been waiting for Murchison to put me through. I think I've got something."

"Shoot."

"La Bresca talked to his mother on the phone about five minutes ago."

"In English or Italian?"

"English. He told her he was expecting a call from Dom Di Fillippi. That could be our man, no?"

"Yeah, it looks like he is," Willis said.

"He told his mother to say he'd meet Di Fillippi on his lunch hour at the corner of Cathedral and Seventh."

"Has Di Fillippi called yet?"

"Not yet. This was just five minutes ago, Hal."

"Right. What time did he say they'd meet?"

"Twelve-thirty."

"Twelve-thirty, corner of Cathedral and Seventh."

"Right," Brown said.

"We'll have somebody there."

"I'll call you back," Brown said. "I've got another customer."

In five minutes, Brown rang the squadroom again. "That was Di Fillippi," he said. "Mrs. La Bresca gave him the message. Looks like pay dirt at last, huh?"

"Maybe," Willis said.

From where Meyer and Kling sat in the Chrysler sedan parked on Cathedral Street, they could clearly see Tony La Bresca waiting on the corner near the bus stop sign. The clock on top of the Catholic church dominating the intersection read twelve-twenty. La Bresca was early and apparently impatient. He paced the pavement anxiously, lighting three cigarettes in succession, looking up at the church clock every few minutes, checking the time against his own wrist watch.

"This has got to be it," Kling said.

"The payoff of the burley joint summit meeting," Meyer said.

"Right. La Bresca's going to tell old Dom he's in for a three-way split. Then Calooch'll decide whether or not they're going to dump him in the river."

"Six-to-five old Dom gets the cement block."

"I'm not a gambling man," Kling said.

The church clock began tolling the half-hour. The chimes rang out over the intersection. Some of the lunch hour pedestrians glanced up at the bell tower. Most of them hurried past with their heads ducked against the cold.

"Old Dom seems to be late," Meyer said.

"Look at old Tony," Kling said. "He's about ready to take a fit."

"Yeah," Meyer said, and chuckled. The car heater was on, and he was snug and cozy and drowsy. He did not envy La Bresca standing outside on the windy corner.

"What's the plan?" Kling said.

"As soon as the meeting's over, we move in on old Dom."

"We ought to pick up *both* of them," Kling said.

"Tell me what'll stick."

"We heard La Bresca planning a job, didn't we? That's Conspiracy to Commit, Section 580."

"Big deal. I'd rather find out what he's up to and then catch him in the act."

"If he's in with the deaf man, he's *already* committed two crimes," Kling said. "And very big ones at that."

"*If* he's in with the deaf man."

"You think he is?"

"No."

"I'm not sure," Kling said.

"Maybe old Dom'll be able to tell us."

"If he shows."

"What time is it?"

"Twenty to," Kling said.

They kept watching La Bresca. He was pacing more nervously now, slapping his gloved hands against his sides to ward off the cold. He was wearing the same beige car coat he had worn the day he'd picked up the lunch pail in the park, the same green muffler wrapped around his throat, the same thick-soled workman's shoes.

"Look," Meyer said suddenly.

"What is it?"

"Across the street. Pulling up to the curb."

"Huh?"

"It's the blond girl, Bert. In the same black Buick!"

"How'd *she* get into the act?"

Meyer started the car. La Bresca had spotted the Buick and was walking toward it rapidly. From where they sat, the detectives could see the girl toss her long blond hair and then lean over to open the front door for him. La Bresca got into the car. In a moment, it gunned away from the curb.

"What do we do now?" Kling asked.

"We follow."

"What about Dom?"

"Maybe the girl's taking La Bresca to see him."

"And maybe not."

"What can we lose?" Meyer asked.

"We can lose Dom," Kling said.

"Just thank God they're not walking," Meyer said, and pulled the Chrysler out into traffic.

This was the oldest part of the city. The streets were narrow, the buildings crowded the sidewalks and gutters, pedestrians crossed at random, ignoring the lights, ducking around moving vehicles with practiced ease, nonchalant to possible danger.

"Like to give them all tickets for jaywalking," Meyer mumbled.

"Don't lose that Buick," Kling cautioned.

"You think I'm new in this business, Sonny?"

"You lost that same car only last week," Kling said.

"I was on *foot* last week."

"They're making a left turn," Kling said.

"I see them."

The Buick had indeed made a left turn, coming out onto the wide tree-lined esplanade bordering the River Dix. The river was icebound shore to shore, a phenomenon that had happened only twice before in the city's history. Devoid of its usual busy harbor traffic, it stretched toward Calm's Point like a flat Kansas plain, a thick cover of snow uniformly hiding the ice below. The naked trees along the esplanade bent in the strong wind that raced across the river. Even the heavy Buick seemed struggling to move through the gusts, its nose swerving every now and again as the blonde fought the wheel. At last, she pulled the car to the curb and killed the engine. The esplanade was silent except for the roaring of the wind. Newspapers flapped into the air like giant headless birds. An empty wicker-wire trash barrel came rolling down the center of the street.

A block behind the parked Buick, Meyer and Kling sat and looked through the windshield of the unmarked police sedan. The wind howled around the automobile, drowning out the calls that came from the radio. Kling turned up the volume.

"What now?" he asked.

"We wait," Meyer said.

"Do we pick up the girl when they're finished talking?" Kling asked.

"Yep."

"You think she'll know anything?"

"I hope so. She must be in on it, don't you think?"

"I don't know. Calucci was talking about splitting the take up the middle. If there're three people in it already . . ."

"Well, then maybe she's old Dom's girl."

"Substituting for him, you mean?"

"Sure. Maybe old Dom suspects they're going to dump him. So he sends his girl to the meeting while he's safe and sound somewhere, strumming his old rhythm guitar."

"That's possible," Kling said.

"Sure, it's possible," Meyer said.

"But then, *anything's* possible."

"That's a very mature observation," Meyer said.

"Look," Kling said. "La Bresca's getting out of the car."

"Short meeting," Meyer said. "Let's hit the girl."

As La Bresca went up the street in the opposite direction, Meyer and Kling stepped out of the parked Chrysler. The wind almost knocked them off their feet. They ducked their heads against it and began running, not wanting the girl to start the car and take off before they reached her, hoping to prevent a prolonged automobile chase through the city. Up ahead, Meyer heard the Buick's engine spring to life.

"Let's *go*!" he shouted to Kling, and they sprinted the last five yards to the car, Meyer fanning out into the gutter, Kling pulling open the door on the curb side.

The blonde sitting behind the wheel was wearing slacks and a short gray coat. She turned to look at Kling as he pulled open the door, and Kling was suprised to discover that she wasn't wearing makeup and that her features were rather heavy and gross. As he blinked at her in amazement, he further learned that she was sporting what looked like a three-day old beard stubble on her chin and on her cheeks.

The door on the driver's side snapped open.

Meyer took one surprised look at the "girl" behind the wheel and then immediately said, "Mr. Dominick Di Fillippi, I presume?"

Dominick Di Fillippi was very proud of his long blond hair.

In the comparative privacy of the squadroom, he combed it often, and explained to the detectives that guys belonging to a group had to have an image, you dig? Like all the guys in his group, they all looked different, you dig? Like the drummer wore these Ben

Franklin eyeglasses, and the lead guitar player combed his hair down in bangs over his eyes, and the organist wore red shirts and red socks, you dig, all the guys had a different image. The long blond hair wasn't exactly his own idea, there were lots of guys in other groups who had long hair, which is why he was growing the beard to go with it. His beard was a sort of reddish-blond, he explained, he figured it would look real tough once it grew in, give him his own distinct image, you dig?

"Like what's the beef," he asked, "what am I doing inside a police station?"

"You're a musician, huh?" Meyer asked.

"You got it, man."

"That's what you do for a living, huh?"

"Well, like we only recently formed the group."

"How recently?"

"Three months."

"Play any jobs yet?"

"Yeah. Sure."

"When?"

"Well, we had like auditions."

"Have you ever actually been *paid* for playing anywhere?"

"Well, no, man, not yet. Not actually. I mean, man, even The Beatles had to start *someplace*, you know."

"Yeah."

"Like, man, they were playing these crumby little cellar joints in Liverpool, man, they were getting maybe a farthing a night."

"What the hell do you know about farthings?"

"Like it's a saying."

"Okay, Dom, let's get away from the music business for a little while, okay? Let's talk about *other* kinds of business, okay?"

"Yeah, let's talk about why I'm in here, okay?"

"You'd better read him the law," Kling said.

"Yeah," Meyer said, and went through the Miranda-Escobedo bit. Di Fillippi listened intently. When Meyer was finished, he nodded his blond locks and said, "I can get a lawyer if I want one, huh?"

"Yes."

"I want one," Di Fillippi said.

"Have you got anyone special in mind, or do you want us to get one for you?"

"I got somebody in mind," Di Fillippi said.

While the detectives back at the squadroom fuzzily and fussily waited for Di Fillippi's lawyer to arrive, Steve Carella, now ambulatory, decided to go down to the fourth floor to visit Patrolman Genero.

Genero was sitting up in bed, his wounded leg bandaged and rapidly healing. He seemed surprised to see Carella.

"Hey," he said, "this is a real honor, I mean it. I'm really grateful to you for coming down here like this."

"How's it going, Genero?" Carella asked.

"Oh, so-so. It still hurts. I never thought getting shot could hurt. In the movies, you see these guys get shot all the time, and they just fall down, but you never get the impression it hurts."

"It hurts, all right," Carella said, and smiled. He sat on the edge of Genero's bed. "I see you've got a television in here," he said.

"Yeah, it's the guy's over in the next bed." Genero's voice fell to a whisper. "He never watches it. He's pretty sick, I think. He's either sleeping all the time or else moaning. I don't think he's going to make it, I'll tell you the truth."

"What's wrong with him?"

"I don't know. He just sleeps and moans. The nurses are in here day and night, giving him things, sticking him with needles, it's a regular railroad station, I'm telling you."

"Well, that's not so bad," Carella said.

"What do you mean?"

"Nurses coming in and out."

"Oh no, that's *great!*" Genero said. "Some of them are pretty good-looking."

"How'd this happen?" Carella asked, and nodded toward Genero's leg.

"Oh, you don't know, huh?" Genero said.

"I only heard you were shot."

"Yeah," Genero said, and hesitated. "We were chasing this suspect, you see. So as he went past me, I pulled my revolver to fire a warning shot." Genero hesitated again. "That was when I got it."

"Tough break," Carella said.

"Well, you got to expect things like that, I suppose. If you expect to make police work your life's work, you got to expect things like that in your work," Genero said.

"I suppose so."

"Well, sure, look what happened to you," Genero said.

"Mmm," Carella said.

"Of course, you're a detective," Genero said.

"Mmm," Carella said.

"Which is sort of understandable."

"What do you mean?"

"Well, you expect detectives to get in trouble more than ordinary patrolmen, don't you? I mean, the ordinary patrolman, the run-of-the-mill patrolman who doesn't expect to make police work his life's work, well, you don't *expect* him to risk his life trying to apprehend a suspect, do you?"

"Well," Carella said, and smiled.

"Do you?" Genero persisted.

"Everybody starts out as a patrolman," Carella said gently.

"Oh, sure. It's just you think of a patrolman as a guy directing traffic or helping kids cross the street or taking information when there's been an accident, things like that, you know? You never figure he's going to risk his life, the run-of-the-mill patrolman, anyway."

"Lots of patrolmen get killed in the line of duty," Carella said.

"Oh, sure, I'm sure. I'm just saying you don't *expect* it to happen."

"To your*self*, you mean."

"Yeah."

The room was silent.

"It sure hurts," Genero said. "I hope they let me out of here soon, though. I'm anxious to get back to duty."

"Well, don't rush it," Carella said.

"When are *you* getting out?"

"Tomorrow, I think."

"You feel okay?"

"Oh yeah, I feel fine."

"Broke your ribs, huh?"

"Yeah, three of them."

"Your nose, too."

"Yeah."

"That's rough," Genero said, "But, of course, you're a detective."

"Mmm," Carella said.

"I was up the squadroom the other day," Genero said, "filling in for the guys when they came here to visit you. This was before the shooting. Before I got it."

"How'd you like that madhouse up there?" Carella said, and smiled.

"Oh, I handled it okay, I guess," Genero said. "Of course, there's a lot to learn, but I suppose that comes with actual practice."

"Oh, sure," Carella said.

"I had a long talk with Sam Grossman . . ."

"Nice fellow, Sam."

". . . yeah, at the lab. We went over those suspect notes together. Nice fellow, Sam," Genero said.

"Yeah."

"And then some kid came in with another one of those notes, and I held him there till the guys got back. I guess I handled it okay."

"I'm sure you did," Carella said.

"Well, you've got to be conscientious about it if you expect to make it your life's work," Genero said.

"Oh, sure," Carella said. He rose, winced slightly as he planted his weight, and then said, "Well, I just wanted to see how you were getting along."

"I'm fine, thanks. I appreciate your coming down."

"Oh, well," Carella said, and smiled, and started for the door.

"When you get back," Genero said, "give my regards, huh?" Carella looked at him curiously. "To all the guys," Genero said. "Cotton, and Hal, and Meyer and Bert. All of us who were on the plant together."

"Oh, sure."

"And thanks again for coming up . . ."

"Don't mention it."

". . . Steve," Genero ventured as Carella went out.

Di Fillippi's lawyer was a man named Irving Baum.

He arrived at the squadroom somewhat out of breath and the first thing he asked was whether the detectives had advised his client of his rights. When assured that Di Fillippi had been constitutionally protected, he nodded briefly, took off his brown Homburg and heavy brown overcoat, placed both neatly across Meyer's desk, and then asked the detectives what it was all about. He was a pleasant-looking man, Baum, with white hair and mustache, sympathetic brown eyes, and an encouraging manner of nodding when anyone spoke, short little nods that seemed to be signs of agreement. Meyer quickly told him that it was not the police intention to book Di Fillippi for anything, but merely to solicit information from him. Baum could see no reason why his client should not co-operate to the fullest extent. He nodded to Di Fillippi and then said, "Go ahead, Dominick, answer their questions."

"Okay, Mr. Baum," Di Fillippi said.

"Can we get your full name and address?" Meyer said.

"Dominick Americo Di Fillippi, 365 North Anderson Street, Riverhead."

"Occupation."

"I already told you. I'm a musician."

"I beg your pardon," Baum said. "Were you questioning him *before* I arrived?"

"Steady, counselor," Meyer said. "All we asked him was what he did for a living."

"Well," Baum said, and tilted his head to one side as though considering whether there had been a miscarriage of justice. "Well," he said, "go on, please."

"Age?" Meyer asked.

"Twenty-eight."

"Single? Married?"

"Single."

"Who's your nearest living relative?"

"I beg your pardon," Baum said, "but if you merely intend to solicit information, why do you need these statistics?"

"Mr. Baum," Willis said, "you're a lawyer, and you're here with him, so stop worrying. He hasn't said anything that'll send him to jail. Not yet."

"This is routine, counselor," Meyer said. "I think you're aware of that."

"All right, all right, go on," Baum said.

"Nearest living relative?" Meyer repeated.

"My father. Angelo Di Fillippi."

"What's he do?"

"He's a stonemason."

"Hard to find good stonemasons today," Meyer said.

"Yeah."

"Dom," Willis said, "what's your connection with Tony La Bresca?"

"He's a friend of mine."

"Why'd you meet with him today?"

"Just friendly."

"It was a very short meeting," Willis said.

"Yeah, I guess it was."

"Do you always go all the way downtown just to talk to someone for five minutes?"

"Well, he's a friend of mine."

"What'd you talk about?"

"Uh music," Di Fillippi said.

"What about music?"

"Well uh he's got a cousin who's gonna get married soon, so he wanted to know about our group."

"What'd you tell him?"

"I told him we were available."

"When's this wedding coming off?"

"The uh sometime in June."

"When in June?"

"I forget the exact date."

"Then how do you know you'll be available?"

"Well, we ain't got no jobs for June, so I know we'll be available."

"Are you the group's business manager?"

"No."

"Then why'd La Bresca come to you?"

"Because we're friends, and he heard about the group."

"So that's what you talked about. His cousin's wedding."

"Yes, that's right."

"How much did you tell him it would cost?"

"I said uh it uh seventy dollars."

"How many musicians are there in the group?"

"Five."

"How much is that a man?" Meyer asked.

"It's uh seventy uh divided by five."

"Which is how much?"

"That's uh well five into seven is one and carry the two, five into twenty is uh four, so that comes to fourteen dollars a man."

"But you didn't know that when you asked for the seventy, did you?"

"Yes, sure I knew it."

"Then why'd you have to do the division just now?"

"Just to check it, that's all."

"So you told La Bresca you'd be available, and you told him it would cost seventy dollars, and then what?"

"He said he'd ask his cousin, and he got out of the car."

"That was the extent of your conversation with him?"

"That was the extent of it, yes."

"Couldn't you have discussed this on the telephone?"

"Sure, I guess so."

"Then why didn't you?"

"Well, I like to see Tony every now and then, he's a good friend of mine."

"So you drove all the way downtown to see him."

"That's right."

"How much did you lose on that championship fight?"

"Oh, not much."

"*How* much?"

"Ten bucks or so. How do *you* know about that?"

"Wasn't it more like fifty?"

"Well, maybe, I don't remember. How do you know this?" He turned to Baum. "How do they know this?" he asked the lawyer.

"How do you know this?" Baum asked.

"Well, counselor, if it's all right with you," Meyer said, "*we'll* ask the questions, unless you find something objectionable."

"No, I think everything's been proper so far, but I *would* like to know where you're going."

"I think that'll become clear," Meyer said.

"Well, Detective Meyer, I think I'd like to know right *now* what this is all about, or I shall feel compelled to advise my client to remain silent."

Meyer took a deep breath. Willis shrugged in resignation.

"We feel your client possesses knowledge of an impending crime," Meyer said.

"What crime?"

"Well, if you'll permit us to question him . . ."

"No, not until you answer me," Baum said.

"Mr. Baum," Willis said, "we can book him for Compounding, Section 570 of the Penal Law, or we can book him for . . ."

"Just a moment, young man," Baum said. "Would you mind explaining that?"

"Yes, sir, we have reason to believe that your client has been promised money or other property to conceal a crime. Now that's either a felony or a misdemeanor, sir, depending on what the crime is he's agreed to conceal. I think you know that, sir."

"And what's this crime he's agreed to conceal?"

"We might also be able to book him for Conspiracy, Section 580, if he's actually *involved* in this planned crime."

"Do you have definite knowledge that a crime is to take place?" Baum asked.

"We have reasonable knowledge, sir, yes, sir."

"You realize, do you not, that no agreement amounts to a conspiracy unless some act *beside* such agreement is done to effect the object thereof?"

"Look, Mr. Baum," Meyer said, "this isn't a court of law, so let's not argue the case right here and now, okay? We're not going to book your client for anything provided he co-operates a little and answers . . ."

"I hope I didn't detect a threat in that statement," Baum said.

"Oh, for Christ's sake," Meyer said, "we know that a man named Anthony La Bresca and another man named Peter Calucci are planning to commit a crime, misdemeanor or felony we don't know which, on March fifteenth. We also have very good reason to believe that your client here knows *exactly* what they're up to and has demanded money from them to keep such knowledge or information from reaching the police. Now, Mr. Baum, we don't want to pull in La Bresca and Calucci for conspiracy because (a) it wouldn't stick without that 'act' you were talking about, and (b) we might end up with only a misdemeanor, depending on what they've cooked up. As I'm sure you know, if they've planned the crime of murder, kidnaping, robbery One, selling narcotics, arson or extortion, and if they've committed some act other than their agreement to pull the job, each of them is guilty of a felony. And as I'm sure you also know, some very big officials in this city were recently murdered, and the possibility exists that La Bresca and Calucci are somehow involved and that this crime they've planned may have to do with extortion or murder, or both, which would automatically make the conspiracy a felony. As you can see, therefore, we're not after your client *per se*, we're merely trying to prevent a crime. So can we cut all the legal bullshit and get a little co-operation from you, and especially from him?"

"It seems to me he's been co-operating splendidly," Baum said.

"It seems to me he's been lying splendidly," Meyer said.

"Considering what's involved here . . ." Baum started.

"Mr. Baum, could we please . . .?"

". . . I think you had better charge Mr. Di Fillippi with whatever it is you have in mind. We'll let the courts settle the matter of his guilt or innocence."

"While two hoods pull off their job, right?"

"I'm not interested in the entrapment of two hood-lums," Baum said. "I'm advising my client to say nothing further, in accordance with the rights granted to him under . . ."

"Thanks a lot, Mr. Baum."

"Are you going to book him, or not?"

"We're going to book him," Meyer said.

"For what?"

"Compounding a crime, Section 570 of the Penal Law."

"Very well, I suggest you do that with reasonable dispatch," Baum said. "It seems to me he's been held in custody an extremely long time as it is. I know you're aware . . ."

"Mr. Baum, we're aware of it inside out and backwards. Take him down, Hal. Charge him as specified."

"Hey, wait a minute," Di Fillippi said.

"I suggest that you go with them," Baum said. "Don't worry about a thing. Before you're even arraigned, I'll have contacted a bail bondsman. You'll be back on the street . . ."

"Hey, wait one goddamn minute," Di Fillippi said. "What if those two guys go ahead with . . .?"

"Dominick, I advise you to remain silent."

"Yeah? What can I get for this 'compounding,' whatever the hell it is?"

"Depends on what they do," Meyer said.

"Dominick . . ."

"If they commit a crime punishable by death or by life imprisonment you can get five years. If they commit . . ."

"What about a holdup?" Di Fillippi asked.

"Dominick, as your attorney, I must again strongly advise you . . ."

"What about a holdup?" Di Fillippi said again.

"Is that what they've planned?" Meyer said.

"You didn't answer me."

"If they commit a robbery, and you take money from them to conceal the crime, you can get three years in prison."

"Mmm," Di Fillippi said.

"Will you answer some questions for us?"

"Will you let me go if I do?"

"Dominick, you don't have to . . ."

"Do *you* want to go to prison for three years?" Di Fillippi asked.

"They have no case, they're . . ."

"No? Then how do they know the job's coming off on March fifteenth? Where'd they get *that*? Some little birdie whisper it in their ear?"

"We've leveled with you, Dominick," Willis said, "and believe me, we wouldn't have brought any of this out in the open if we didn't have plenty to go on. Now you can either help us or we can book you and take you down for arraignment and you'll have an arrest record following you for the rest of your life. What do you want to do?"

"That's coercion!" Baum shouted.

"It may be coercion, but it's also fact," Willis said.

"I'll tell you everything I know," Di Fillippi said.

He knew a lot, and he told it all.

He told them that the holdup was set for eight o'clock

on Friday night, and that the victim was to be the owner
of a tailor shop on Culver Avenue. The reason the hit had
been scheduled for that particular night and time was
that the tailor, a man named John Mario Vicenzo, usually
packed up his week's earnings then and took them home
with him in a small metal box, which box his wife Laura
carried to the Fiduciary Trust early Saturday morning.
The Fiduciary Trust, as it happened, was the only bank
in the neighborhood that was open till noon on Saturday,
bank employees being among those who did not like to
work on weekends.

John Mario Vicenzo (or John the Tailor as he was
known to the people along Culver Avenue) was a man in
his early seventies, an easy mark. The take would be
enormous, Di Fillippi explained, with more than enough
for everyone concerned even if split three ways. The
plan was to go into the shop at ten minutes to eight, just
before John the Tailor drew the blinds on the plate glass
window fronting the street. La Bresca was to perform
that task instead, and then he was to lock the front door
while Calucci forced John the Tailor at gun point into the
back room, where he would tie him and leave him bound
and helpless on the floor near the pressing machine.
They would then empty the cash register of the money
that had been piling up there all week long, and take off.
John the Tailor would be left dead or alive depending on
how cooperative he was.

Di Fillippi explained that he'd overheard all this one
night in the pizzeria on South Third, La Bresca and
Calucci sitting in a booth behind him and not realizing
they were whispering a little too loud. At first he'd been

annoyed by the idea of two Italians knocking over a place owned by another Italian, but then he figured What the hell, it was none of his business; the one thing he'd never done in his life was rat on anybody. But that was before the fight, and the bet that left him broke. Desperate for a little cash, he remembered what he'd heard them discussing and figured he'd try to cut himself in. He didn't think there'd be too much static from them because the take, after all, was a huge one, and he figured they'd be willing to share it.

"Just how much money is involved here?" Willis asked.

"Oh, man," Di Fillippi said, rolling his eyes, "there's at least four hundred bucks involved here, maybe even more."

A LOT OF THINGS HAPPENED ON WEDNESDAY.

It was discovered on Wednesday, for example, that somebody had stolen the following items from the squad room:

A typewriter.

Six ballpoint pens.

An electric fan.

A thermos jug.

A can of pipe tobacco, and

Four bars of soap.

Nobody could figure out who had done it.

Not even Steve Carella, who had been released from the hospital and who was very delicately walking around with his ribs taped, could figure out who had done it. Some of the squadroom wits suggested that Carella, being an invalid and all, should be assigned to the Great

Squadroom Mystery, but Lieutenant Byrnes decided it would be better to assign him to the tailor shop stakeout instead, together with Hal Willis. At twelve noon that Wednesday, the pair headed crosstown to John the Tailor's shop.

But before then a lot of other things happened, it was certainly a busy Wednesday.

At 8:00 A.M., for example, a patrolman walking his beat called in to report that he had found a stiff in a doorway and that it looked to him as if the guy had been burned to death. Which meant that the two fire bugs had struck again sometime during the night, and that something was going to have to be done about them pretty soon before they doused every bum in the city with gasoline. Kling, who took the call, advised the patrolman to stay with the body until he could get a meat wagon over, and the patrolman complained that the doorway and the entire street stank to high heaven and Kling told him that was tough, he should take the complaint to Captain Frick.

At 9:15 A.M., Sadie the Nut came up to tell Willis about the rapist who had tried to steal her virginity the night before. Sadie the Nut was seventy-eight years old, a wrinkled toothless crone who had been protecting her virginity for close to fourscore years now, and who unfailingly reported to the squadroom every Wednesday morning, either in person or by phone, that a man had broken into her tenement flat the night before and tried to tear off her nightgown and rape her. The first time she'd reported this attempted crime some four years back, the police had believed her, figuring they had another Boston Strangler on their hands, only this time right in their own back yard. They immediately initiated an investigation, going so far as to plant Detective Andy Parker in the old lady's apartment. But the following Wednesday morning, Sadie came to the squadroom again to report a second rape attempt—even though Parker had spent an uneventful Tuesday night alert and awake in her kitchen. The squadroom comedians speculated that perhaps Parker himself was the rape artist, a premise Parker found somewhat less than amusing. They all realized by then, of course, that Sadie was a nut, and that they could expect frequent visits or calls from her. They did not realize that the visits or calls would come like clockwork every Wednesday morning, nor that Sadie's fantasy was as fixed and as unvaried as the squadroom itself. Her rapist was always a tall swarthy man who somewhat resembled Rudolph Valentino. He was always wearing a black cape over a tuxedo, white dress shirt, black bow tie, black satin dancing slippers. His pants had buttons on the fly. Five buttons. He always unbuttoned his fly slowly and teasingly, warning Sadie not to scream, he was not going to hurt her, he was (in Sadie's own words) "only going to rapage her." Sadie invariably waited until he had unbuttoned each of the five buttons and taken out his "thing" before she screamed. The rapist would then flee from the apartment, leaping onto the fire escape like Douglas Fairbanks, and swinging down into the back yard.

Her story this Wednesday was the same story she had been telling every Wednesday for the past four years. Willis took down the information and promised they would do everything in their power to bring this insane womanizer to justice. Sadie the Nut left the squadroom pleased and excited, doubtless anticipating next week's nocturnal visit.

At a quarter to ten that morning, a woman came in to report that her husband was missing. The woman was perhaps thirty-five years old, an attractive brunette wearing a green overcoat that matched her Irish eyes. Her face was spanking pink from the cold outside, and she exuded health and vitality even though she seemed quite upset by her husband's disappearance. Upon questioning her, though, Meyer learned that the missing man wasn't her husband at all, he was really the husband of her very best friend who lived in the apartment next door to her on Ainsley Avenue. And upon further questioning, the green-eyed lady explained to Meyer that she and her very best friend's husband had been having "a relationship" (as she put it) for three years and four months, with never a harsh word between them, they were that fond of each other. But last night, when the green-eyed lady's best friend went to play Bingo at the church, the green-eyed lady and the husband had had a violent argument because he had wanted to "do it" (as she again put it) right there in his own apartment on the living-room couch with his four children asleep in the other room, and she had refused, feeling it would not be decent, and he had put on his hat and coat and gone out into the cold. He had not yet returned, and whereas the green-eyed lady's best friend figured he was out having himself a toot, the husband apparently being something of a drinking man, the green-eyed lady missed him sorely and truly believed he had vanished just to spite her, had she known he would do something like that she certainly would have let him have his way, you know how men are.

Yes, Meyer said.

So whereas the wife felt it would not be necessary to report him missing and thereby drag policemen into the situation, the green-eyed lady feared he might do something desperate, having been denied her favors, and was therefore asking the law's assistance in locating him and returning him to the bosom of his family and loved ones, you know how men are.

Yes, Meyer said again.

So he took down the information, wondering when it was that he'd last attempted to lay Sarah on the living-room couch with his own children asleep in their respective rooms, and realized that he had *never* tried to lay Sarah on the living-room couch. He decided that he would try to do it tonight when he got home, and then he assured the green-eyed lady that they would do everything in their power to locate her best friend's husband, but that probably there was nothing to worry about, he had probably gone to spend the night with a friend.

Yes, that's *just* what I'm worried about, the green-eyed lady said.

Oh, Meyer said.

When the green-eyed lady left, Meyer filed the information away for future use, not wanting to bug the Bureau of Missing Persons prematurely. He was beginning to type up a report on a burglary when Detective Andy Parker came into the squadroom with Lewis the Pickpocket. Parker was laughing uncontrollably, but Lewis did not seem too terribly amused. He was a tall slender man with a bluish cast to his jowls, small sharp penetrating blue eyes, thinning sandy-colored hair. He was wearing a beige trench coat and brown leather gloves, and he carried an umbrella in the crook of his arm and scowled at everyone in the squadroom as Parker continued laughing uproariously.

"Look who *I* got!" Parker said, and burst into a choking, gasping fit.

"What's so special?" Meyer said. "Hello, Lewis, how's business?"

Lewis scowled at Meyer. Meyer shrugged.

"Best pickpocket in the precinct!" Parker howled. "Guess what happened?"

"What happened?" Carella asked.

"I'm standing at the counter in Jerry's, you know? The luncheonette?"

"Yeah?"

"Yeah, with my back to the door, you know? So guess what?"

"What?"

"I feel somebody's hand in my pocket, fishing around for my wallet. So I grab the hand by the wrist, and I whip around with my gun in my other hand, and guess who it is?"

"Who is it?"

"It's Lewis!" Parker said, and began laughing again. "The best pickpocket in the precinct, he chooses a *detective* for a mark!"

"I made a mistake," Lewis said, and scowled.

"Oh, man, you made a *big* mistake!" Parker bellowed.

"You had your back to me," Lewis said.

"Lewis, my friend, you are going to prison," Parker said gleefully, and then said, "Come on down, we're going to book you before you try to pick Meyer's pocket there."

"I don't think it's funny," Lewis said, and followed Parker out of the squadroom, still scowling.

"*I* think it's pretty funny," Meyer said.

A man appeared at the slatted rail divider just then, and asked in hesitant English whether any of the policemen spoke Italian. Carella said that he did, and invited the man to sit at his desk. The man thanked him in Italian and took off his hat, and perched it on his knees when he sat, and then began telling Carella his story. It seemed that somebody was putting garbage in his car.

"*Rifiuti?*" Carella asked.

"*Sì, rifiuti,*" the man said.

For the past week now, the man went on, someone had been opening his car at night and dumping garbage all over the front seat. All sorts of garbage. Empty tin cans and dinner leftovers and apple cores and coffee grounds, everything. All over the front seat of the car.

"*Perchè non lo chiude a chiave?*" Carella asked.

Well, the man explained, he *did* lock his car every night, but it didn't do any good. Because the way the garbage was left in it the first time was that *quello porco* broke the side vent and opened the door that way in order to do his dirty work. So it didn't matter if he continued to lock the car, the befouler continued to open the door by sticking his hand in through the broken flap window, and then he dumped all his garbage on the front seat, the car was beginning to stink very badly.

Well, Carella said, do you know of anyone who might want to put garbage on your front seat?

No, I do not know of anyone who would do such a filthy thing, the man said.

Is there anyone who has a grudge against you? Carella asked.

No, I am loved and respected everywhere in the world, the man said.

Well, Carella said, we'll send a man over to check it out.

"*Per piacere,*" the man said, and put on his hat, and shook hands with Carella, and left the squadroom.

The time was 10:33 A.M.

At 10:35 A.M., Meyer called Raoul Chabrier down at the district attorney's office, spent a delightful three minutes chatting with Bernice, and was finally put through to Chabrier himself.

"Hello, Rollie," Meyer said, "what'd you find out?"

"About what?" Chabrier said.

"About the book I called to . . ."

"Oh."

"You forgot," Meyer said flatly.

"Listen," Chabrier said, "have *you* ever tried handling two cases at the same time?"

"Never in my life," Meyer said.

"Well, it isn't easy, believe me. I'm reading law on one of them, and trying to get a brief ready on the other.

You expect me to worry about some goddamn novel at the same time?"

"Well . . ." Meyer said.

"I know, I know, I know," Chabrier said, "I promised."

"Well . . ."

"I'll get to it. I promise you again, Meyer. I'm a man who never breaks his word. Never. I promised you, and now I'm promising you again. What was the title of the book?"

"*Meyer Meyer*," Meyer said.

"Of course, *Meyer Meyer*, I'll look into it immediately. I'll get back to you, I promise. Bernice," he shouted, "make a note to get back to Meyer!"

"When?" Meyer said.

That was at 10:39.

At five minutes to eleven, a tall blond man wearing a hearing aid and carrying a cardboard carton walked into the Hale Street Post Office downtown. He went directly to the counter, hefted the carton onto it, and shoved it across to the mail clerk. There were a hundred sealed and stamped envelopes in the carton.

"These all going to the city?" the clerk asked.

"Yes," the deaf man replied.

"First class?"

"Yes."

"All got stamps?"

"Every one of them."

"Right," the clerk said, and turned the carton over, dumping the envelopes onto the long table behind him. The deaf man waited. At eleven A.M., the mail clerk began running the envelopes through the cancellation machine.

The deaf man went back to the apartment, where Rochelle met him at the door.

"Did you mail off your crap?" she asked.

"I mailed it," the deaf man said, and grinned.

John the Tailor wasn't having any of it.

"I no wanna cops in my shop," he said flatly and unequivocally and in somewhat fractured English.

Carella patiently explained, in English, that the police had definite knowledge of a planned holdup to take place on Friday night at eight o'clock but that it was the lieutenant's idea to plant two men in the rear of the shop starting tonight in case the thieves changed their minds and decided to strike earlier. He assured John the Tailor that they would unobtrusively take up positions behind the hanging curtain that divided the front of the shop from the rear, out of his way, quiet as mice, and would move into action only if and when the thieves struck.

"*Lei è pazzo!*" John the Tailor said in Italian, meaning he thought Carella was crazy. Whereupon Carella switched to speaking Italian, which he had learned as a boy and which he didn't get much chance to practice these days except when he was dealing with people like the man who had come in to complain about the garbage in his car, or people like John the Tailor, who was suddenly very impressed with the fact that Carella, like himself, was Italian.

John the Tailor had once written a letter to a very popular television show, complaining that too many of the Italians on that show were crooks. He had seventy-four people in his immediate family, all of them living here in the United States, in this city, for most of their lives, and none of them were criminals, all of them were honest, hard-working people. So why should the television make it seem that all Italians were thieves? He had received a letter written by some programming assistant, explaining that not all the criminals on the show were Italians, some of them were Jews and Irish, too. This had not mollified John the Tailor, since he was quite intelligent and capable of understanding the basic difference between the two statements *Not all Italians are criminals* and *Not all criminals are Italians*. So it was very pleasant to have an Italian cop in his shop, even if it meant having to put up with strangers in the back behind the curtain. John the Tailor did not like strangers, even if they were Italian cops. Besides, the other stranger, the short one, definitely was *not* Italian, God knew what *he* was!

The tailor shop did a very thriving business, though Carella doubted it brought in anything near four hundred dollars a week, which was apparently La Bresca's and Calucci's estimate of the take. He wondered why either of the two men would be willing to risk a minimum of ten and a maximum of thirty years in prison, the penalty for first-degree robbery, when all they could hope to gain for their efforts was four hundred dollars. Even granting them the minimum sentence, and assuming they'd be out on parole in three-and-a-half, that came to about a hundred and fifteen dollars a year, meager wages for *any* occupation.

He would never understand the criminal mind.

He could not, for example, understand the deaf man at all.

There seemed to be something absolutely lunatic about the enormous risk he had taken, a gamble pitting fifty thousand dollars against possible life imprisonment. Now surely a man of his intelligence and capabilities must have known that the city wasn't going to reach into its treasury and plunk down fifty thousand dollars soley because someone threatened murder. The odds against such a payoff were staggering, and any shrewd manipulator of odds would have realized this. The deaf man, then, had not *expected* to be paid, he had *wanted* to kill the deputy mayor, as he had earlier killed the parks commissioner. But why? Whatever else the deaf man happened to be, Carella did not figure him for a thrill killer. No, he was a hardheaded businessman taking a calculated risk. And businessmen don't take risks unless there's at least some hope of a payoff. The deaf man had asked for five grand at first, and been refused, and committed murder. He had next asked for fifty grand, knowing full well he'd be refused again, and had again committed murder. He had then advised the newspapers of his unsuccessful extortion attempts, and had since remained silent.

So where was the payoff?

It was coming, baby, of that Carella was sure.

In the meantime, he sat in the back of John the Tailor's shop and wondered how much a good pressing machine operator earned.

Mr. Carl Wahler
1121 Marshall Avenue
Isola

Dear Mr. Wahler:

If you treat this letter as a joke, you will die.
These are the facts. Read them carefully. They can
save your life.
1) Parks Commissioner Cowper ignored a warning and
   was killed.
2) Deputy Mayor Scanlon ignored a warning and was
   killed.
3) JMV is next. He will be killed this Friday night.

What does all this have to do with you?
1) This is your warning. It is your only warning. There
   will be no further warnings. Remember that.

2) You are to withdraw five thousand dollars in small,
unmarked bills from your account.

3) You will be contacted by telephone sometime within
the next week. The man you speak to will tell you
how and when and where the money is to be delivered.

4) If you fail to meet this demand, you too will be
killed. <u>Without warning</u>.

<u>Do not entertain false hopes!</u>

The police could not save Cowper or Scanlon, although
sufficiently forewarned. They will not be able to save
JMV, either. What chance will <u>you</u> have unless you
pay? What chance will you have when we strike
<u>without warning</u>?

Get the money. You will hear from us again. Soon.

The letters were delivered to a hundred homes on
Thursday. The deaf man was very cheerful that morning.
He went whistling about his apartment, contemplating
his scheme again and again, savoring its more refined
aspects, relishing the thought that one hundred very
wealthy individuals would suddenly be struck with
panic come Saturday morning.

By five o'clock tonight, he could reasonably assume
that most of the men receiving his letter would have read
it and formed at least some tentative opinion about it. He
fully expected some of them to glance cursorily at it,
crumple it into a ball, and immediately throw it into the
garbage. He also expected a handful, the paranoid
fringe, to call the police at once, or perhaps even visit
their local precinct, letter in hand, indignantly de-

manding protection. *That* part of his plan was particularly beautiful, he felt. The mayor was being warned, yes, but oh so indirectly. He would learn about the threat on his life only because some frightened citizens would notify the police.

And tomorrow night, forewarned, the mayor would nonetheless die.

Six months ago when the deaf man had begun the preliminary work on his scheme, several rather interesting pieces of information had come to light. To begin with, he had learned that anyone desiring to know the exact location of the city's underground water pipes need only apply to the Department of Water Supply in Room 1720 of the Municipal Building, where the maps were available for public scrutiny. Similarly, maps of the city's underground sewer system were obtainable at the Department of Public Works in the main office of that same building. The deaf man, unfortunately, was not interested in either water pipes or sewers. He was interested in electricity. And he quickly learned that detailed maps of the underground power lines were *not*, for obvious reasons, open to the public for inspection. Those maps were kept in the Maps and Records Bureau of the Metropolitan Light & Power Company, worked on by an office staffed largely by draftsmen. Ahmad had been one of those draftsmen.

The first map he delivered to the deaf man was titled "60 Cycle Network Area Designations and Boundaries Lower Isola," and it showed the locations of all the area substations in that section of the city. The area that specifically interested the deaf man was the one labeled "Cameron Flats." The mayor's house was on the corner

of South Meridian and Vanderhof, in Cameron Flats.
The substation serving South Meridian and Vanderhof
was marked with a cross in a circle, and was designated
"No. 3 South Meridian." Into this substation ran high-
voltage supply cables. ("They're called feeders," Ahmad
said) from a switching station elsewhere on the transmission system. It would be necessary to destroy those
supply cables if the mayor's house was to be thown into
darkness on the night of his murder.

The second map Ahmad delivered was titled "System
Ties" and was a detailed enlargement of the feeder systems supplying any given substation. The substation on
the first map had been labeled "No. 3 South Meridian."
By locating this on the more detailed map, the deaf man
was able to identify the number designation of the
feeder: 65CA3. Which brought him to the third pilfered
map, simply and modestly titled "65CA3," and subtitled
"Location South Meridian Substation." This was a rather
long, narrow diagram of the route the feeder traveled
below the city's streets, with numbers indicating the
manholes that provided access to the cables. 65CA3
passed through eleven manholes on its meandering underground travels from the switching station to the substation. The deaf man chose a manhole approximately a
half-mile from the mayor's house and wrote down its
number: M3860-120'SSC-CENT.

The last map, the crucial one, was titled "Composite
Feeder Plate" and it pinpointed the manhole exactly.
M3860 was located on Faxon Drive, a hundred and
twenty feet south of the southern curb of Harris, in the
center of the street—hence the 120'SSC-CENT. The

high-voltage cables passing through that concrete manhole were five feet below the surface of the street protected by a three-hundred-pound manhole cover.

Tomorrow night, Ahmad, Buck, and the deaf man
would lift that cover, and one of Buck's bombs would effectively take care of the cables.

And then . . .

Ahh, then . . .

The really beautiful part was still ahead, and the deaf
man smiled as he contemplated it.

He could visualize the mayor's house at 10 P.M. tomorrow night, surrounded by policemen and detectives
on special assignment, all there to protect the honorable
JMV from harm. He could see himself driving a black
sedan directly to the curb in front of the darkened brick
structure, a police flashlight picking out the gold lettering on the front door, Metropolitan Light & Power
Company (pressure-sensitive letters expertly applied by
Ahmad to both front doors of the car, cost eight cents
per letter at Studio Art Supply, total expenditure $4.80).
He could see the car doors opening. Three men step out
of it. Two of them are wearing workmen's coveralls
(Sears, Roebuck, $6.95 a pair). The third is wearing the
uniform of a police sergeant, complete with a citation
ribbon pinned over the shield on the left breast (The-
atrical Arts Rentals, $10.00 per day, plus a $75.00 de-
posit) and the yellow sleeve patch of the Police
Department's Emergency Service ($1.25 at the Civic
Equipment Company, across the street from Headquarters).

"Who's there?" the policeman on duty asks. His

flashlight scans the trio. Buck, in the sergeant's uniform, steps forward.

"It's all right," Buck says. "I'm Sergeant Pierce, Emergency Service. These men are from the electric company. They're trying to locate that power break."

"Okay, Sergeant," the cop answers.

"Everything quiet in there?" Buck asks.

"So far, Sarge."

"Better check out their equipment," Buck says. "I don't want any static on this later."

"Good idea," the cop says. He swings his flashlight around. Ahmad opens the tool box. There is nothing in it but electrician's tools: a test light, a six-foot rule, a brace, four screwdrivers, a Stillson wrench, a compass saw, a hacksaw, a hammer, a fuse puller, wire skinners, wire cutters, gas pliers, Allen wrenches, friction tape, rubber tape . . . "Okay," the cop says, and turns to the deaf man. "What's that you're carrying?"

"A volt-ohm meter," the deaf man answers.

"Want to open it for me?"

"Sure," the deaf man says.

The testing equipment is nothing more than a black leather case perhaps twelve inches long by eight inches wide by five inches deep. When the deaf man unclasps and raises the lid, the flashlight illuminates an instrument panel set into the lower half of the case, level with the rim. Two large dials dominate the panel, one marked "Volt-Ohm Meter," the other marked "Ammeter." There are three knobs spaced below the dials. Factory-stamped lettering indicates their use: the two end knobs are marked "Adjuster," and the one in the middle is marked

"Function." Running vertically down the left-hand side of the panel are a series of jacks respectively marked 600V, 300V, 150V, 75V, 30V, and Common. Flanking the dials on the right-hand side of the plate there are similiar jacks marked 60 Amps, 30 Amps, 15 Amps, 7.5 Amps, 3 Amps, and Common. Another jack and a small bulb are below the second adjuster knob, and they are collectively marked "Leakage Indicator." In bold factory-stamped lettering across the length of the tester are the words "Industrial Analyzer."

"Okay," the cop says, "you can close it."

The deaf man snaps the lid of the case shut, fastens the clasp again.

"I'll take them inside," Buck says.

"Right, Sarge," the cop says, and the trio goes up the walk to the house, where they are stopped by a detective at the front door.

"Sergeant Pierce, Emergency Service," Buck says. "These men are from the electric company, here to check that power failure."

"Right," the detective says.

"I'll stick with them," Buck says, "but I don't want no other responsibility."

"What do you mean?"

"Well, if the mayor trips and breaks his ankle while they're on the premises, I don't want no static from my captain."

"We'll keep the mayor far away from you," the detective says, and smiles.

"Okay, where you guys want to start?" Buck asks. "The basement?"

They go into the house. There are battery-powered lights set up, but for the most part the house is dim, the figures moving through it are uncertainly defined. The three men start in the basement, going through the motions of checking out circuits. They go through every room of the house, never once seeing the mayor in the course of their inspection. In the master bedroom, the deaf man shoves the testing equipment under the huge double bed, ostensibly searching for a leak at the electrical outlet. When he walks out of the room, he is no longer carrying anything. The "Industrial Analyzer" is on the floor under the mayor's bed.

That analyzer, with its factory-sleek assortment of dials, knobs, jacks, and electrical terminology is real—but nonetheless fake. There *is* no testing equipment behind those meters, the interior of the box has been stripped bare. Hidden below the instrument panel, set to go off at 2 A.M., there is only another of Buck's bombs.

Tomorrow night, the mayor would die.

And on Saturday morning, the uncommitted would commit. They would open their newspapers and read the headlines, and they would know the letter was for real, no opportunist could have accurately predicted the murder without having engineered it and executed it himself. They would take the letter from where they had casually put it, and they would read it once again, and they would fully comprehend its menace now, fully realize the absolute terror inherent in its words. When one was faced with the promise of unexpected death, was five thousand dollars really so much to invest? Not a man on that list of one hundred earned less than

$200,000 a year. They had all been carefully researched, the original list of four hundred and twenty names being cut and revised and narrowed down to only those who seemed the most likely victims, those to whom losing five thousand dollars at a Las Vegas crap table meant nothing, those who were known to have invested in speculative stocks or incoming Broadway plays—those, in short, who would be willing to gamble five thousand dollars in hope of salvation.

They will pay us, the deaf man thought.

Oh, not all of them, certainly not all of them. But enough of them. Perhaps a few more murders are in order, perhaps some of those sleek fat cats on the list will have to be eliminated before the rest are convinced, but they *will* be convinced, and they *will* pay. After the murder tomorrow night, after that, when they know we're not fooling, they will pay.

The deaf man suddenly smiled.

There should be a very large crowd around City Hall starting perhaps right this minute, he thought.

It will be an interesting weekend.

"You hit the nail right on the head," Lieutenant Byrnes said to Steve Carella. "He's going for the mayor next."

"He'll never get away with it," Hawes said.

"He'd better *not* get away with it," Byrnes said. "If he succeeds in knocking off the mayor, he'll be picking up cash like it's growing in the park. How many of these letters do you suppose he's mailed?"

"Well, let's try to figure it," Carella said. "First he

warned the parks commissioner and demanded five thousand dollars. Next the deputy mayor, and a demand for fifty thousand. Now he tells us he'll kill the mayor this Friday night. So if the escalation carries through, he should be bucking for ten times fifty thousand, which is five hundred thousand. If we divide that by—"

"Forget it," Byrnes said.

"I'm only trying to figure out the mathematics."

"What's mathematics got to do with JMV getting killed?"

"I don't know," Carella said, and shrugged. "But it seems to me if we can figure out the progression, we can also figure out what's *wrong* with the progression."

Byrnes stared at him.

"I'm trying to say it just isn't enough for this guy to knock off the mayor," Carella said.

"It isn't, huh? Knocking off the mayor seems like *more* than enough to me."

"Yeah, but not for somebody like the deaf man. He's too proud of his own cleverness." Carella looked at the letter again. "Who's this man Carl Wahler?" he asked.

"A dress manufacturer, lives downtown in Stewart City, 17th Precinct. He brought the letter in there this morning. Captain Bundy thought we'd want to see it. Because of our involvement with the previous murders."

"It seems to fit right in with the pattern, doesn't it?" Hawes said. "He announced the other murders, too."

"Yes, but there's something missing," Carella said.

"What?"

"The personal angle. He started this in the 87th, a little vendetta for fouling him up years ago, when he was planting bombs all over the goddamn city to divert attention from his bank job. So why's he taking it *out* of the 87th all at once? If he knocks off the mayor, nobody looks foolish but the special police assigned to his protection. *We're* off the hook, home free. And that's what I can't understand. That's what's wrong with the pattern."

"The pattern seems pretty clear to me," Byrnes said. "If he can get to JMV after advertising it, what chance will anybody have *without* warning? Look at how many times he says that in his letter. Without warning, without warning."

"It still bothers me," Carella said.

"It shouldn't," Byrnes said. "He's spelled it out in black and white. The man's a goddamn *fiend*."

The instant reaction of both Hawes and Carella was to laugh. You don't as a general rule hear cops referring to criminals as "fiends," even when they're child molesters and mass murderers. That's the sort of language reserved for judges or politicians. Nor did Byrnes usually express himself in such colorful expletives. But whereas both men felt a definite impulse to laugh out loud, one look at Byrnes' face stifled any such urge. The lieutenant was at his wit's end. He suddenly looked very old and very tired. He sighed heavily, and said, "How do we stop him, guys?" and he sounded for all the world like a freshman quarterback up against a varsity team with a three-hundred-pound line.

"We pray," Carella said.

Although James Martin Vale, the mayor himself, was a devout Episcopalian, he decided that afternoon that

he'd best do a lot more than pray if his family was to
stay together.

So he called a top-level meeting in his office at City
Hall (a meeting to which Lieutenant Byrnes was not invited), and it was decided that every precaution would
be taken starting right then to keep "the deaf man" (as
the men of the 87th insisted on calling him) from carrying out his threat. JMV was a man with a charming
manner and a ready wit, and he managed to convince
everyone in the office that he was more concerned about
the people of his city than he was about his own safety.
"We've got to save my life only so that this man won't
milk hard-earned dollars from the people of this great
city," he said. "If he gets away with this, they'll allow
themselves to be extorted. That's why I want protection."

"Your Honor," the district attorney said, "if I may
suggest, I think we should extend protection beyond the
Friday night deadline. I think if this man succeeds in
killing you anytime in the near future, the people of this
city'll think he's made good his threat."

"Yes, I think you're right," JMV said.

"Your Honor," the city comptroller said, "I'd like to
suggest that you cancel all personal appearances at least
through April."

"Well, I don't think I should go into complete seclu-
sion, do you?" JMV asked, mindful of the fact that this
was an election year.

"Or at least *curtail* your personal appearances," the
comptroller said, remembering that indeed this was an
election year, and remembering, too, that he was on the
same ticket as His Honor the Mayor JMV.

"What do you think, Slim?" JMV asked the police commissioner.

The police commissioner, a man who was six feet four inches tall and weighed two hundred and twenty-five pounds, shifted his buttocks in the padded leather chair opposite His Honor's desk, and said, "I'll cover you with cops like fleas," a not particularly delicate simile, but one which made its point nonetheless.

"You can count on however many men you need from my squad," the district attorney said, mindful that two of his most trusted detectives had been blown to that big Police Academy in the sky only days before.

"I would like to suggest," the city's medical examiner said, "that you undergo a complete physical examination as soon as this meeting is concluded."

"Why?" JMV asked.

"Because the possibility exists, Your Honor, that you've already been poisoned."

"Well," JMV said, "that sounds a bit farfetched."

"Your Honor," the medical examiner said, "an accumulation of small doses of poison administered over a period of time can result in death. Since we're dealing with a man who has obviously evolved a long-term plan . . ."

"Yes, of course," JMV said, "I'll submit to examination as soon as you wish. Maybe you can clear up my cold at the same time," he said charmingly, and grinned charmingly.

"Your Honor," the president of the city council said, "I suggest we have each of the city's vehicles inspected thoroughly and at once. I am remembering, sir, the bomb placed in . . ."

"Yes, we'll have that done at once," the district attorney said hastily.

"Your Honor," the mayor's press secretary said, "I'd like to suggest that we suppress all news announcements concerning your whereabouts, your speaking engagements, and so on, until this thing blows over."

"Yes, that's a good idea," JMV said, "but of course I won't be venturing too far from home in any case, will I, Stan?" he said, and grinned charmingly at the district attorney.

"No, sir, I'd advise your becoming a homebody for the next month or so," the district attorney said.

"Of course, there may be a bomb in this office right this minute," the police commissioner said tactlessly, causing everyone to fall suddenly silent. Into the silence came the loud ticking of the wall clock, which was a little unnerving.

"Well," JMV said charmingly, "perhaps we ought to have the premises searched, as well as my home. If we're to do this right, we'll have to take every precaution."

"Yes, sir," the district attorney said.

"And, of course, we'll have to do everything in our power meanwhile to locate this man, this deaf man."

"Yes, sir, we're doing everything in our power right now," the police commissioner said.

"Which is what?" JMV asked, charmingly.

"He's got to make a mistake," the police commissioner said.

"And if he doesn't?"

"He's *got* to."

"But in the meantime," JMV asked, "do you have any leads?"

"Police work," the commissioner said, "is a combination of many seemingly unconnected facets that suddenly jell," and frowned, suspecting that his metaphor hadn't quite come off. "There are a great many accidents involved in police work, and we consider these accidents a definite contributing factor in the apprehension of criminals. We will, for example, arrest a man on a burglary charge, oh, six or seven months from now, and discover in questioning him that he committed a homicide during the commission of another crime, oh four or five months ago."

"Well," JMV said charmingly, "I hope we're not going to have to wait six or seven months for our man to make a mistake while committing another crime."

"I didn't mean to sound so pessimistic," the commissioner said. "I was merely trying to explain, Your Honor, that a lot of police work dovetails past and present and future. I have every confidence that we'll apprehend this man within a reasonable length of time."

"Hopefully before he kills me," JMV said, and grinned charmingly. "Well," he said, "if there's nothing further to discuss, perhaps we can set all these precautionary measures into motion. I'll be happy to see your doctor, Herb, whenever you want to send him in."

"Meanwhile, I'll get in touch with the Bomb Squad," the police commissioner said, rising.

"Yes, that's probably the first thing to do," JMV said,

rising. "Gentlemen, thank you for your time and your valuable suggestions. I'm sure everything will work out fine."

"You'll have men here in the next two or three minutes," the district attorney promised.

"Thank you, Stan," the mayor said, "I certainly appreciate your concern."

The men filed out of the mayor's office, each of them assuring him once again that he would be amply protected. The mayor thanked each of them charmingly and individually, and then sat in the big padded leather chair behind his desk and stared at the ticking wall clock.

Outside, it was beginning to snow.

The snow was very light at first.

It drifted from the sky lazily and uncertainly, dusting the streets and the sidewalks with a thin fluffy powder. By eight P.M. that night, when Patrolman Richard Genero was discharged from Buena Vista Hospital, the snow was beginning to fall a bit more heavily, but it presented no major traffic problems as yet, especially if—like Genero's father—one had snow tires on his automobile. Their ride home was noisy but uneventful. Genero's mother kept urging her son to talk to the captain, and Genero's father kept telling her to shut up. Genero himself felt healthy and strong and was anxious to get back to work, even though he'd learned he would start his tour of duty on the four-to-midnight tomorrow. He had also learned, however, that Captain Frick, in consideration for his recent wound, was not asking him to walk a beat for the next week or so. Instead, he would be

riding shotgun in one of the RMP cars. Genero considered this a promotion.

Of sorts.

The snow continued to fall.

13

F<small>RIDAY.</small>

The city was a regular tundra, you never saw so much snow in your life unless you happened to have been born and raised in Alaska, and then probably not. There was snow on everything. There was snow on roofs and walls and sidewalks and streets and garbage cans and automobiles and flowerpots, and even on people. Boy, what a snowfall. It was worse than the Blizzard of '88, people who didn't remember the Blizzard of '88 were saying. His Honor the Mayor JMV, as if he didn't have enough headaches, had to arrange with the Sanitation Department for the hiring of 1200 additional temporary employees to shovel and load and dump the snow into the River Dix, a job estimated to cost five hundred and eight thousand four hundred dollars and to consume the better part of a full week—if it didn't snow again.

The men began working as soon as the snow stopped. It did not stop until three-thirty P.M., fifteen minutes before Genero began riding the RMP car, an hour and a half before Willis and Carella took their posts in the rear of the tailor shop. The city had figured on working their snow people in three continuous shifts, but they hadn't figured on the numbing cold that followed the storm and lowered the rate of efficiency, a biting frigid wave that had come down from Canada or someplace. Actually, nobody cared *where* it had come from, they merely wished it would continue going, preferably out to sea, or down to Bermuda, or even all the way to Florida; do it to *Julia*, everyone was thinking.

There was no doing it to Julia that day.

The cold gripped the city and froze it solid. Emergency snow regulations had gone into effect at noon, and by four P.M. the city seemed deserted. Most large business offices were closed, with traffic stalled to a standstill and buses running only infrequently. Alternate-side-of-the-street parking had been suspended, but stranded automobiles blocked intersections, humped with snow like igloos on an arctic plain. The temporary snowmen fought the cold and the drifted snow, huddled around coal fires built in empty gasoline drums, and then manned their shovels again while waiting dump trucks idled, exhaust pipes throwing giant white plumes into the bitter dusk. The lamppost lights came on at five P.M., casting isolated amber circles on the dead white landscape. A fierce relentless wind howled across avenue and street as the leaden sky turned dark and darker and black.

• • •

Sitting cozy and warm in the back room of John the Tailor's shop, playing checkers with Hal Willis (and losing seven games in a row since it turned out that Willis had belonged to the checkers club in high school, an elite group calling itself *The Red and The Black*), Carella wondered how he would get home after La Bresca and Calucci hit the shop.

He was beginning to doubt that they would hit at all. If there was one thing he did not understand, of course, it was the criminal mind, but he was willing to venture a guess that no self-respecting crook would brave the snow and the cold outside on a night like this. It would be different if the job involved a factor that might change in a day or so, like say ten million dollars of gold bullion to be delivered at a precise moment on a specific day, making it necessary to combine pinpoint timing with insane daring, but no such variable was involved in this penny-ante stickup. The men had cased the shop and learned that John the Tailor carried his week's earnings home in a metal box every Friday night after closing. He had doubtless been performing this same chore every Friday night for the past seven thousand years, and would continue to do it without variation for the next thousand. So, if not *this* Friday night, what are you doing *next* Friday, John? Or, better yet, why not wait until May, when the trees are budding and the birds are singing, and a man can pull off a little felony without the attendant danger of frostbite?

But assuming they did hit tonight, Carella thought as he watched Willis double-jump two of his kings, assuming they *did* hit, and assuming he and Willis behaved as expected, made the capture, and then called in for a squad car with chains, how would he get home to his wife and children after La Bresca and Calucci were booked and put away for the night? His own car had snow tires, but not chains, and he doubted if the best snow tires made would mean a damn on that glacier out there. A possibility, of course, was that Captain Frick would allow one of the RMPs to drive him home to Riverhead, but using city property for transporting city employees was a practice heavily frowned upon, especially in these days of strife when deaf people were running around killing city officials.

"King me," Willis said.

Carella snorted and kinged him. He looked at his watch. It was seven-twenty. If La Bresca and Calucci hit as expected, there was little more than a half-hour to go.

In Pete Calucci's rented room on North Sixteenth, he and La Bresca armed themselves. John the Tailor was seventy years old, a slight stooped man with graying hair and failing eyes, but they were not taking any chances with him that night. Calucci's gun was a Colt Government Model .45, weighing thirty-nine ounces and having a firing capacity of seven, plus one in the chamber. La Bresca was carrying a Walther P-38, which he had bought from a fence on Dream Street, with eight slugs in the magazine and another in the chamber. Both guns were automatics. The Walther was classified as a medium-power pistol whereas the Colt, of course, was a heavy gun with greater power. Each was quite capable of leaving John the

Tailor enormously dead if he gave them any trouble. Neither man owned a holster. Calucci put his pistol into the right-hand pocket of his heavy overcoat. La Bresca tucked his into the waistband of his trousers.

They had agreed between them that they would not use the guns unless John the Tailor began yelling. It was their plan to reach the shop by ten minutes to eight, surprise the old man, leave him bound and gagged in the back room, and then return to Calucci's place. The shop was only five minutes away, but because of the heavy snow, and because neither man owned an automobile, they set out at seven twenty-five.

They both looked very menacing, and they both felt quite powerful with their big guns. It was a shame nobody was around to see how menacing and powerful they looked and felt.

In the warm snug comfort of the radio motor patrol car, Patrolman Richard Genero studied the bleak and windswept streets outside, listening to the clink of the chains on the rear wheel tires, hearing the two-way short wave radio spewing its incessant dialogue. The man driving the RMP was a hair bag named Phillips, who had been complaining constantly from the moment they'd begun their shifts at three forty-five P.M. It was now seven-thirty, and Phillips was still complaining, telling Genero he'd done a Dan O'Leary this whole past week, not a minute's breather, man had to be crazy to become a cop, while to his right the radio continued its oblivious spiel, Car Twenty-one, Signal thirteen, This is Twenty-one, Wilco, Car Twenty-eight, signal . . .

"This reminds me of Christmas," Genero said.

"Yeah, some Christmas," Phillips said, "I *worked* on Christmas day, you know that?"

"I meant, everything white."

"Yeah, everything white," Phillips said. "Who needs it?"

Genero folded his arms across his chest and tucked his gloved hands into his armpits. Phillips kept talking. The radio buzzed and crackled. The skid chains clinked like sleigh bells.

Genero felt drowsy.

Something was bothering the deaf man.

No, it was not the heavy snow which had undoubtedly covered manhole number M3860, a hundred and twenty feet south of the southern curb of Harris, in the center of Faxon Drive, no, it was not that. He had prepared for the eventuality of inclement weather, and there were snow shovels in the trunk of the black sedan idling at the curb downstairs. The snow would merely entail some digging to get at the manhole, and he was allowing himself an extra hour for that task, no, it was not the snow, it was definitely not the snow.

"What is it?" Buck whispered. He was wearing his rented police sergeant's uniform, and he felt strange and nervous inside the blue garment.

"I don't know," Ahmad answered. "Look at the way he's pacing."

The deaf man was indeed pacing. Wearing electrician's coveralls, he walked back and forth past the desk in one corner of the room, not quite muttering, but certainly wagging his head like an old man contemplating the sorry state of the world. Buck, perhaps emboldened by the bravery citation on his chest, finally approached him and said, "What's bothering you?"

"The 87th," the deaf man replied at once.

"What?"

"The 87th, the 87th," he repeated impatiently. "What difference will it make if we kill the mayor? Don't you see?"

"No."

"They get away clean," the deaf man said. "We kill JMV, and *who* suffers, will you tell me that?"

"Who?" Buck asked.

"*Not* the 87th, that's for sure."

"Look," Buck said gently, "we'd better get started. We've got to dig down to that manhole, we've got to . . ."

"So JMV dies, so what?" the deaf man asked. "Is money everything in life? Where's the pleasure?"

Buck looked at him.

"Where's the *pleasure*?" the deaf man repeated. "If JMV—" He suddenly stopped, his eyes widening. "JMV," he said again, his voice a whisper. "JMV!" he shouted excitedly, and went to the desk, and opened the middle drawer, and pulled out the Isola telephone directory. Quickly, he flipped to the rear section of the book.

"What's he doing?" Ahmad whispered.

"I don't know," Buck whispered back.

"*Look* at this!" the deaf man shouted. "There must be hundreds of them, *thousands* of them!"

"Thousands of what?" Buck asked.

The deaf man did not reply. Hunched over the directory, he kept turning pages, studying them, turning more pages. "Here we are," he mumbled, "no, that's no good . . . let's see . . . here's another one . . . no, no . . . just a second . . . ahh, good . . . no, that's all the way downtown . . . let's see, let's see . . . here . . . no . . ." mumbling to himself as he continued to turn pages, and finally shouting "Culver Avenue, *that's* it, that'll do it!" He picked up a pencil, hastily scribbled onto the desk pad, tore the page loose, and stuffed it into the pocket of his coveralls. "Let's go!" he said.

"You ready?" Buck asked.

"I'm ready," the deaf man said, and picked up the volt-ohm meter. "We promised to get JMV, didn't we?" he asked.

"We sure did."

"Okay," he said, grinning. "We're going to get *two* JMVs—and one of them's in the 87th Precinct!"

Exuberantly, he led them out of the apartment.

The two young men had been prowling the streets since dinnertime. They had eaten in a delicatessen off Ainsley and then had stopped to buy a half-gallon of gasoline in the service station on the corner of Ainsley and Fifth. The taller of the two young men, the one carrying the open can of gasoline, was cold. He kept telling the shorter one how cold he was. The shorter one said *everybody* was cold on a night like this, what the hell did he expect on a night like this?

The taller one said he wanted to go home. He said they wouldn't find nobody out on a night like this, anyway, so what was the use walking around like this in the cold? His feet were freezing, he said. His hands were cold too. Why don't *you* carry this fuckin' gas a while? he said.

The shorter one told him to shut up.

The shorter one said this was a perfect night for what they had to do because they could probably find maybe two guys curled up together in the same hallway, didn't that make sense?

The taller one said he wished *he* was curled up in a hallway someplace.

They stood on the street corner arguing for a few minutes, each of them yelling in turn, and finally the taller one agreed to give it another ten minutes, but that was all. The shorter one said Let's try it for another half-hour, we bound to hit pay dirt, and the taller one said No, ten minutes and that's it, and the shorter one said You fuckin' idiot, I'm telling you this is a good night for it, and the taller one saw what was in his eyes, and became afraid again and said Okay, okay, but only a half-hour, I mean it, Jimmy, I'm really cold, really.

You look like you're about to start crying, Jimmy said.

I'm cold, the other one said, that's all.

Well, come on, Jimmy said, we'll find somebody and make a nice fire, huh? A nice warm fire.

The two young men grinned at each other.

Then they turned the corner and walked up the street toward Culver Avenue as Car Seventeen, bearing Phillips and Genero, clinked by on its chained tires sounding like sleigh bells.

● ● ●

It was difficult to tell who was more surprised, the cops or the robbers.

The police commissioner had told His Honor the Mayor JMV that "a lot of police work dovetails past and present and future," but it was fairly safe to assume he had nothing too terribly philosophical in mind. That is, he probably wasn't speculating on the difference between illusion and reality, or the overlap of the dream state and the workaday world. That is, he probably wasn't explaining time continua or warps, or parallel universes, or coexisting systems. He was merely trying to say that there are a lot of accidents involved in police work, and that too many cases would never get solved if it weren't for those very accidents. He was trying to tell His Honor the Mayor JMV that sometimes cops get lucky.

Carella and Willis got very lucky on that night of March fifteenth at exactly ten minutes to eight.

They were watching the front of the shop because Dominick Di Fillippi (who had never ratted on anybdy in his life) had told them the plan was to go into the shop at ten minutes to eight, just before John the Tailor drew the blinds on the plate glass window fronting the street. La Bresca was to perform that task instead, Di Fillippi had further said, and then he was to lock the front door while Calucci forced John the Tailor at gun point into the back room. In Di Fillippi's ardent recital, there had been a lot of emphasis, real or imagined, on the *front* of the shop. So everyone had merely assumed (as who wouldn't?) that La Bresca and Calucci would come in through the front door, open the door, ting-a-ling would go the bell, shove their guns into John the Tailor's face, and then go about their dirty business. It is doubtful that the police even *knew* there was a back door to the shop.

La Bresca and Calucci knew there was a back door.

They kicked that door in at precisely seven-fifty, right on schedule, kicked it in noisily and effectively, not caring whether or not they scared John the Tailor out of ten years' growth, knowing he would rush to the back of the shop to see what the hell was happening, knowing he would run directly into two very large pistols.

The first thing they saw was two guys playing checkers.

The first thing La Bresca said was, "Fuzz!"

He knew the short guy was fuzz because he had been questioned by him often enough. He didn't know who the other guy was, but he reasoned that if you saw *one* mouse you probably had fifty, and if you saw one *cop* you probably had a thousand, so the place was probably crawling with cops, they had stepped into a very sweet little trap here—and that was when the curtain shot back and the front door of the shop burst open.

It was also when all the overlapping confusion started, the past, present, and future jazz getting all mixed up so that it seemed for a tense ten seconds as if seven movies were being projected simultaneously on the same tiny screen. Even later, much later, Carella couldn't quite put all the pieces together; everything happened too fast and too luckily, and he and Willis had very little to do with any of it.

The first obvious fact that crackled up Carella's spine and into his head was that he and Willis had been caught cold. Even as he rose from his chair, knocking it over backwards, even as he shouted, "Hal, behind you!" and reached for his revolver, he knew they'd been caught cold, they were staring into the open muzzles of two high caliber guns and they would be shot dead on the spot. He heard one of the men shout, "Fuzz!" and then he saw both guns come up level at the same time, and too many last thoughts crowded into his head in the tick of a second. Willis whirled, knocking checkerboard and checkers to the floor, drawing his gun, and suddenly John the Tailor threw back the curtain separating the rear of the shop from the front, and the front door of the shop burst open in the same instant.

John the Tailor later said he had run back to see what the noise was, throwing the curtain between the two rooms, and then whirling to see what Carella only later saw, three men standing in the front doorway of his shop, all of them holding pistols.

This was what La Bresca and Calucci must have seen as well, looking through the now open curtain directly to the front door. And whereas they must have instantly known they had caught the back-room cops cold, they now recognized the threat of the three other cops standing in the front door, all of them with pistols in their fists and kill looks on their faces. The three men weren't cops, but La Bresca and Calucci didn't know that. The sergeant standing in the doorway shouted, "Fuzz!" meaning he thought La Bresca and Calucci were fuzz, but La Bresca and Calucci merely thought he was announcing his own arrival. So they began shooting. The three men in the door, facing what they

too thought was a police trap, opened fire at the same
time. John the Tailor threw himself to the floor. Carella
and Willis, recognizing a good healthy crossfire when
they saw one, tried to flatten themselves against the wall.
In the flattening process, Willis slipped on one of the
fallen checkers and went tumbling to the floor, bullets
spraying over his head.

Carella's gun was in his hand now. He leveled it at
the front door because he had taken a good look at one
of the men standing there firing into the back room, and
whereas the man was not wearing his hearing aid, he
was tall and blond and Carella recognized him at once.
He aimed carefully and deliberately. The gun bucked in
his hand when he pulled off the shot. He saw the deaf
man clutch for his shoulder and then half-stumble, half-
turn toward the open doorway. Someone screamed behind Carella, and he turned to see La Bresca falling over
the pressing machine, spilling blood onto the white
padding, and then four more shots exploded in the tiny
shop and someone grunted, and there were more shots,
Willis was up and firing, and then there was only smoke,
heavy smoke that hung on the air in layers, the terrible
nostril-burning stink of cordite, and the sound of John
the Tailor on the floor, praying softly in Italian.

"Outside!" Carella shouted, and leaped the counter
dividing the shop, slipping in a pool of blood near the
sewing machine, but regaining his footing and running
coatless into the snow.

There was no one in sight.

The cold was numbing.

It hit his naked gun hand immediately, seemed to wed flesh to steel.

A trail of blood ran from the shop door across the white snow stretching endlessly into the city.

Carella began following it.

The deaf man ran as fast as he could, but the pain in his shoulder was intolerable.

He could not understand what had happened.

Was it possible they had figured it out? But no, they couldn't have. And yet, they'd been there, waiting. How *could* they have known? How could they *possibly* have known when he *himself* hadn't known until fifteen minutes ago?

There had been at least twenty-five pages of "V" listings in the Isola directory, with about 500 names to a page, for a combined total of some 12,500 names. He had not counted the number of first names beginning with the letter "J," but there seemed to be at least twenty or thirty on every page, and he had actually gone through *eleven* names with the initials "JMV," the same initials as His Honor the Mayor James Martin Vale, before coming to the one on Culver Avenue.

How could they have known? How could they have pinpointed the tailor shop of John Mario Vicenzo, the final twist of the knife, a JMV located within the very confines of the 87th? It's impossible, he thought. I left nothing to chance, it should have worked, I should have got them both, there were no wild cards in the deck, it should have worked.

There were *still* some wild cards in the deck.

• • •

"Look," Jimmy said.

The taller boy, the one carrying the gasoline can, lifted his head, squinted against the wind, and then ducked it immediately as a fiercer gust attacked his face. He had seen a tall blond man staggering off the pavement and into the center of the snowbound street.

"Drunk as a pig," Jimmy said beside him. "Let's get him, Baby."

The one called Baby nodded bleakly. Swiftly, they ran toward the corner. The wind was stronger there, it struck them with gale force as they turned onto the wide avenue. The vag was nowhere in sight.

"We lost him," Baby said. His teeth were chattering, and he wanted to go home.

"He's got to be in one of these hallways," Jimmy said. "Come on, Baby, it's fire time."

From where Genero sat in the RMP car, he could see the empty windswept avenue through a frost-free spot on the windshield, snow devils ascending with each fresh gust of wind, hanging signs clanging and flapping, an eerie graveyard sound rasping at the windows of the automobile. The avenue was deserted, the snow locked the street from sidewalk to sidewalk, lights burned behind apartment windows like warming fires in a primeval night.

"What's that?" he said suddenly.

"What's what?" Phillips asked.

"Up ahead. Those two guys."

"Huh?" Phillips said.

"They're trying doors," Genero said. "Pull over."

"Huh?"

"Pull over and cut your engine!"

He could hear them talking on the sidewalk outside, he could hear their voices coming closer and closer. He lay in the hallway with his shoulder oozing blood, knowing he had to climb those steps and get to the roof, get from this building to the next one, jump rooftops all night long if he had to, but first rest, just rest, just rest a little, rest before they opened the door and found him, how had they got to him so fast? Were there policemen all over this damn city?

There were too many things he did not understand.

He listened as the voices came closer, and then he saw the doorknob turning.

"Hold it right there!" Genero shouted.

The boys turned immediately.

"Fuzz!" Baby shouted, and dropped the gasoline can, and began running. Genero fired a warning shot over his head, and then belatedly yelled, "Police! Stop or I'll shoot!" and then fired another warning shot. Up the street, where he had parked the RMP at the curb, Phillips was opening the door on the driver's side and unholstering his revolver. Genero fired again, surprised when he saw the running boy drop to the snow. I *got* him! he thought, and then whirled to see the second boy running in the opposite direction, Holy Jesus, he thought, I'm busting up a *robbery* or something! "Halt!" he shouted. "Stop!" and fired into the air, and saw the boy rounding the corner, and immediately ran after him.

He chased Jimmy for three blocks in the snow, pushing through knee-deep drifts, slipping on icy patches, the wind a constant adversary, and finally caught up with him as he was scaling a back-alley fence.

"Hold it right there, Sonny," Genero said, "or I'll put one right up your ass."

Jimmy hesitated astride the fence, debating whether to swing his legs up and over it, or to get down before this trigger-happy bastard really carried out his threat.

Sighing, he dropped to the ground at Genero's feet.

"What seems to be the trouble, Officer?" he asked.

"*Trouble* is right," Genero said. "Get your hands up."

Phillips came puffing into the alley just then. He walked up to Genero like the hair bag he was, shoved him aside, and then pushed Jimmy against the fence while he frisked him. Genero was smart enough to make certain *his* handcuffs were the ones they put on the kid, though there was a moment there when it seemed like a touch-and-go race with Phillips.

By the time they got the kid back to the squad car, by the time they went up the street to ascertain that the other kid was still alive, though barely, by the time they located the hallway door the kids were about to open, by the time they opened that door themselves and flashed their lights into the foyer, all they saw was a puddle of blood on the floor.

The blood continued up the steps.

They followed the spatters to the top floor, directly to the open door of the roof. Genero stepped outside and threw the beam of his flash across the snow.

Bloodstains and footprints led in an erratic trail to the edge of the roof, and from there to the roof beyond, and from there to the rest of the city, or perhaps the rest of the world.

Two blocks away, they found Steve Carella wandering coatless in the snow like Dr. Zhivago or somebody.

THE CLEANUP IN THE TAILOR SHOP WAS A GRUESOME JOB.

La Bresca and Calucci were both dead. The big red-headed man named Buck was also dead. Ahmad was alive and breathing when they carted him off in the meat wagon, but he had taken two slugs in the chest from Calucci's .45, and another in the stomach from La Bresca's Walther. He was gushing blood, and spitting blood, and shivering and mumbling, and they doubted very much if he'd make it to the hospital alive.

Carella was shivering a little himself.

He stood near the radiator in the tailor shop, wrapped in his overcoat, his teeth chattering, and asked John the Tailor how much money there was in the metal box he was taking home.

"Due cento tre dollari," John the Tailor said.

Two hundred and three dollars.

• • •

Ahmad knew the deaf man's name.

"Orecchio," he said, and the nurse wiped blood from his lips. "Mort Orecchio."

"That's not his real name," Willis told him. "Do you know him by any other name?"

"Orecchio," Ahmad repeated. "Mort Orecchio."

"Is there anyone who *might* know his real name?"

"Orecchio," Ahmad repeated.

"Was there anyone else in this with you?"

"The girl," Ahmad said.

"What girl?"

"Rochelle," he said.

"Rochelle what?"

Ahmad shook his head.

"Where can we find her?"

"Three . . . three . . . eight . . . Ha . . . Ha . . . Ha . . ." he said, and died.

He had not died laughing.

He was trying to say 338 Harborside.

They found in Buck's pants pocket a letter addressed to him at 338 Harborside Oval. His full name was Andrew Buckley, and the letter was addressed to him c/o Mr. Mort Orecchio. Carella and Willis hit the apartment and found a pretty brunette girl in lounging pajamas, sitting at the piano playing "Heart and Soul." They waited while she got dressed and then took her to the squad-room, where they questioned her for a half-hour in the presence of a lawyer. The girl told them her name was Rochelle Newell and that she had known the deaf man for only a short time, two or three months. She insisted his name was Mort Orecchio.

"That's not his name," Carella said.

"Yes, that's his name."

"What'd *you* call him?"

"Mort," the girl said.

"What'd you call him in *bed?*" Willis asked suddenly, hoping to surprise her.

"Sweetie," the girl answered.

Jimmy could not stop giggling.

They had just told him that his friend Baby was dead, and yet he could not stop giggling.

"You know the kind of trouble you're in, son?" Meyer asked.

"No, what kind?" Jimmy said, and giggled.

"We're going to book you for homicide."

"It won't stick," Jimmy said, and giggled.

"It'll stick, son," Meyer said. "We got a dying confession from your pal, and it was taken in the presence of a lawyer, and we've got a cop outside who you tried to kill and who'll make a positive identification of both of you. It'll stick, believe me."

"Naw, it won't stick," Jimmy said, and kept giggling.

Meyer figured he was crazy.

Meyer figured Rollie Chabrier was crazy too.

He called at close to midnight.

"This is kind of late, isn't it?" Meyer said. "I was just about to head home."

"Well, I'm still working here at the goddamn office," Chabrier said. "You guys have it easy."

"Well, what is it?" Meyer said.

"About this book," Chabrier said.

"Yeah?"

"You want my advice?"

"Sure, I want your advice. Why do you think I contacted you?"

"My advice is forget it."

"That's some advice."

"Has Steve Carella ever had a book named after him?"

"No, but . . ."

"Has Bert Kling?"

"No."

"Or Cotton Hawes? Or Hal Willis? Or Arthur Brown? Or . . ."

"Look, Rollie . . ."

"You should be flattered," Chabrier said. "Even *I* have never had a book named after me."

"Yeah, but . . ."

"You know how many people go their entire lives and never have books named after them?"

"How many?"

"Millions! You should be flattered."

"I should?"

"Sure. Somebody named a book after you! You're famous!"

"I am?"

"Absolutely. From now to the very end of time, people will be able to go into libraries all over the world

and see your name on a book, Meyer, think of it. On a
book. Meyer Meyer," he said grandly, and Meyer could
almost visualize him spreading his hands as though con-
juring marquee lights. "God, Meyer, you should be
thrilled to death."

"Yeah?" Meyer said.

"I envy you, Meyer. I truly and honestly envy you."

"Gee," Meyer said. "Thanks. Thanks a lot, Rollie.
Really. Thanks a lot."

"Don't mention it," Chabrier said, and hung up.

Meyer went into the men's room to look at himself in
the mirror.

Andy Parker brought the morning papers into the
squadroom at 2:00 A.M.

"You want to read how smart we are?" he said, and
dropped the papers on Kling's desk.

Kling glanced at the headlines.

"Sure," Parker said, "we busted the whole thing wide
open. Nobody can lick *this* team, pal."

Kling nodded, preoccupied.

"Everybody can rest easy now," Parker said. "The
papers tell all about the scheme, and how the ring is
busted, and how none of those hundred marks have to
worry anymore. And all because of the brilliant bulls
of the 87th." He paused and then said, "I bet Genero
gets a promotion out of this. His name's all over the
paper."

Kling nodded and said nothing.

He was pondering the latest development in the Great

Squadroom Mystery. The stolen electric fan, it seemed, had turned up in a hockshop downtown. There had been an apple green fingerprint on its base.

"Now who do you suppose . . ." he started, but Parker had already stretched out in the swivel chair behind his desk, with one of the newspapers over his face.

THE 87TH PRECINCT MYSTERIES
BY ED MCBAIN

☐ **FUZZ**
(0-446-60971-4, $6.50 USA) ($8.99 Can.)

☐ **SHOTGUN**
(0-446-60973-0, $6.50 USA) ($8.99 Can.)

☐ **JIGSAW**
(0-446-60972-2, $6.50 USA) ($8.99 Can.)

☐ **LET'S HEAR IT FOR THE DEAF MAN**
(0-446-60970-6, $6.99 USA) ($9.99 Can.)

☐ **SADIE WHEN SHE DIED**
(0-446-60969-2, $6.99 USA) ($9.99 Can.)

☐ **HAIL, HAIL, THE GANG'S ALL HERE**
(0-446-60968-4, $6.99 USA) ($9.99 Can.)

**AVAILABLE AT A BOOKSTORE NEAR
YOU FROM WARNER BOOKS**